VIRTUE

GENEVIEVE JACK

Carpe Luna Publishing

VIRTUE: FIREBORN WOLVES BOOK 2

BOOKS BY GENEVIEVE JACK

Knight Games Series

The Ghost and The Graveyard, Book 1

Kick the Candle, Book 2

Queen of the Hill, Book 3

Mother May I, Book 4

Knight World Novels

Logan

Fireborn Wolves Series

Vice, Book 1

Virtue, Book 2

Vengeance, Book 3

ONE

"Jason. Jason! Wake up."

Pale fingers shook Jason's shoulder, their perfect French manicure digging into the skin under his Fireborn pack tattoo. He rolled onto his back, passing beneath a curtain of silky blond hair that brushed his cheek from above. The hair cascaded from a perfectly shaped head attached to a perfectly shaped body, with perfectly shaped lips that parted slightly when he opened his eyes. Sarah. Her fair skin seemed to glow in the dim light, making her look as sweet as an angel. But he knew better than to judge this book by its cover. The nail marks down his back proved otherwise. Angel in the daylight, devil between the sheets.

"Mmmm. Haven't you had enough, darling?" he drawled. "Are you going for some kind of a record?" He grabbed her thigh and tried to pull her on top of him. She smiled but slapped his hand away.

"Seriously, you need to get dressed and leave. My cousin is in town. We're meeting for drinks." She bounced from the bed and swept her bra from the floor in one lithe movement, her Fireborn tattoo flashing in the mirror above the dresser.

Jason glanced at his watch; it was only 10:30 p.m. The night had barely begun. "I could join you." He grinned wryly.

She slipped her silky underwear over her hips as her expression tightened. "Are you kidding me?"

"What? Your cousin isn't interested in meeting pack royalty?"

"No, I'm not interested in becoming the latest pack gossip."

"How long have we known each other, Sarah?" Jason propped his head up, eyes tightening in feigned concentration.

"Two years."

"And we… date regularly."

"We bang regularly. In private. With no other expectations."

"I don't see anything wrong with doing something other than bang. We could take our relationship to the next level."

"Don't, Jason. Don't make this something it's not." She shook her head and pulled a flowing apricot dress over her head. "We have an arrangement, not a relationship."

Jason swung his legs over the side of the bed and retrieved his custom-tailored dress shirt from the back of her desk chair. "I've never treated you like an arrangement."

She snorted. "You call me every Thursday. We have sex and then you leave. I know the women of Tuesday and Friday personally, Jason. They are two of my closest friends."

Horrified, he pulled on his Armani slacks with more gusto than necessary. "Are you saying you compare notes about me with your girlfriends?"

She shrugged. "It is what it is."

He stepped in close, tipping his head and giving her a wolfish grin. "You seemed to enjoy our arrangement well enough tonight." As he approached her, his inner wolf woke up and paced inside him, ready for action. She shifted playfully at first, but the moment her wolf recognized his, her body sagged in submission. He caught the base of her lovely head in one hand and slipped the other under the skirt of her dress.

"What exactly do you talk about with Tuesday and Friday?"

"I talk about… I…" He brushed the strip of fabric over her sex, reveling in the wet heat he found there. His mouth hovered over hers. "I talk about how impossible you are to quit," she said in a voice as brittle as dried bones. "How I'll never be able to find a mate because I'll always be Thursday."

He stopped. Pulled back. "You feel like I'm keeping you from finding a mate?"

"What male would mate with a woman who is at the Fireborn prince's beck and call? Even if he didn't have to submit to you, I would. I couldn't say no, even if I wanted to."

"I've never forced you to do anything." He wasn't the alpha after all. He had no metaphysical power over her.

"No. I knew what I was getting into the first time I said yes. Don't pretend you don't realize the effect you have on women. It's okay. I've come to accept this relationship for what it is. Sometimes… I think of it as a service to our pack."

"A service to our pack?" Jason cried, pulling away from her. "A service to our pack!"

"You have a vice. I get it. I don't even want to know what would happen if your wolf wasn't fed regularly. I understand my place in the pack—I'm a willing participant."

"So this is charity sex to you?" With a pensive grunt, Jason fastened his cufflinks. One of his Italian leather loafers was missing. He dropped to his knees and fished it out from under her bed.

She spread her hands, looking frustrated and confused. "How would you characterize our relationship?"

He wedged his foot into the shoe and set his jaw. "Just two people taking solace from an unforgiving world in the safety of each other's arms."

Lips parting, she made a noise deep in her throat like she was going to say something, then turned toward the mirror to reapply her lipstick. Her hand trembled slightly. "I know what I am to you," she said toward the mirror. "And it's cruel of you to tease me with the idea it could be something more."

"Maybe it's time we moved things forward." He shrugged. "Look, this doesn't have to be an arrangement. We can bring it into the light. Go with me to my sister's wedding. I need a date."

She paused, her eyebrows pinching together. "Like be your public date at your sister's royal wedding?"

Swaggering toward her, he flashed his most endearing smile. "Come on, Sarah. It will be fun."

"People will see us. They'll think we're a legitimate couple."

"So what? Let's become a legitimate couple then. Like I said, maybe it's time to move things forward."

A whisper of a smile curved her tightly pressed lips. "Okay…"

Jason clapped his manicured hands together. "Yes!"

She held up one finger, her eyes darting away from him. "I will go to the wedding with you, act as your girlfriend, even look the other way when you inevitably attempt to bed someone else. I know you can't help it."

"Excellent—"

"On one condition."

"What's that, darling?"

"Say my last name."

"Hmm?"

"What's my last name, Jason? We've been screwing every Thursday for two years. Do you know my last name?"

"Of course I do." He bent down to straighten his sock, searching his brain for answers. It was something with a T. Tennison. No, no. Timmerman. No, that wasn't it. Lumberjack. He was picturing a lumberjack. "Timber. Sarah Timber."

She closed her eyes and shook her head. "Hawthorn."

"There it is! I knew it was a tree." He spread his hands.

Touching his cheek gently, she said, "I don't think it's a good idea."

"Sarah…"

"I can see you're going through something, and I hope you find whatever it is you're looking for. But I'm not it." She pressed her lips against his, then backed away and opened her bedroom door. He shrugged into his suit jacket, skimmed his keys off her dresser, and left without another word.

* * *

The Bugatti Jason drove was capable of 260 mph, but he crept along the winding drive that led to the gatehouse of his high-rise condominium at a glacier's pace. His mind was distracted with the evening's conversation and with a nagging ache that had begun at the base of his skull.

"A service to our pack," he repeated grimly. He rubbed the back of his neck. "I need a drink."

An Audi behind him honked impatiently. He waved his arm out the window, motioning for the driver to pass. As the car pulled around, he glimpsed the gray-blue hair of Mrs. Bloomburg. Great. Passed by an octogenarian. Her upturned middle finger goaded him from her window, her engine revving as she left him in her dust. And wasn't that just the icing on the cake to an otherwise disaster of an evening?

The road ended at a gatehouse where a slender redhead asked for his resident card. He held it out to her, then, noticing her tiny waist and pert breasts, snatched it away before she could snag it. She giggled flirtatiously. Game on.

"You must be new here"—he glanced at her badge—"Teresa." Jason smiled in a practiced way, the type of smile an actor might use to convey attraction.

"No... But I usually work days." Her gaze traveled over his car and his suit before settling on his face. She sighed deeply.

Yes, rich and good-looking, darling. He handed her the card again, making sure to brush her fingers with his own, his touch lingering just long enough for her to notice. "Really? Well, I knew there must be some explanation. I never forget a beautiful woman."

He gloried at the slight reddening of her cheeks. An easy blush. He could have some fun with this one.

"Thank you." She handed his card back, her fingers grazing his unnecessarily in the process. "All clear." The barrier lifted.

"What time do you get off?" He managed to load the words *get off* with sexual energy.

"Four in the morning."

"Want to come up for an early morning drink? I'm in the penthouse."

"Won't you be sleeping?"

"Not if you come up."

She smiled sheepishly, her eyes darting to the corner of the small hut she was working in. "Maybe."

Way to play it coy, Teresa.

"There's someone behind you," she said, gesturing with her head.

Jason looked in his rearview mirror to see Mr. Anderson raising his hands in frustration. "Hmm. We wouldn't want Mr. Anderson to dislodge the stick from his ass." She gave a breathy laugh. "Have a nice night." He tipped his head in her general direction and continued to the parking lot. A short ride alone on the elevator and he arrived on the twenty-fifth floor of the Bachman Building, the best piece of real estate available in Carlton City.

A woman he'd met in New York decorated it for him during their torrid affair. She'd insisted on it, tired as she was of staring at his bare white walls. The affair didn't last but the décor did, and it was good enough to earn her a feature in *Architectural Digest*, a consolation prize, he supposed, for his failure to commit.

She'd called it minimalist but welcoming: black stone, white oak floors, gray walls. There was an oatmeal-colored sofa that cost as much as a small village. He rarely sat on it.

He crossed to the fridge, the appliance perfectly masked to appear an extension of the cabinets, and hung his head inside. There was nothing worth eating, but he fished a half-full bottle of Sauvignon Blanc from the shelf and pulled out the cork. "Dinner is served." He retrieved a wineglass from the small bar in his great room. Narrow-bowled, for white wines. He wasn't a barbarian.

Shedding his suit jacket, he took a seat at the designer table off his kitchen and flipped open his laptop. A few hours of work would clear his head. Sure enough, one of his scouts had a start-up he thought was worthy of Jason's attention—a tech company called Spackles with a patent for LED paint. It went on white but could change colors when connected to a power source. Jason clicked the link for background and financials.

Another e-mail popped up, this one from Ryker Vandoren, an owner whose small business Jason had funded only a few months ago. Jason hadn't had high hopes for the project. It was a small occult shop in the vampire district, a niche market for sure and not in line with his usual investment profile. But Ryker had proved persuasive, supernaturally so, and before Jason could think too much about the opportunity, he'd already written the check.

He clicked on the e-mail.

Jason,

Per our agreement, I've transferred to your account 10 percent of my first month's profits. See attached.

Ryker

Attached was a transaction confirmation in the six-figure range. Jason blinked, then logged into his account to double-check the amount. His eyebrows shot up. Perhaps Ryker's shop was a good investment after all.

His phone vibrated on the table. Laina.

"Rehearsal is tomorrow, Friday, seven o'clock. It will take several hours, so make sure you move your, um, appointment to earlier in the day."

"Why hello, sister. It's good to speak with you. Of course I will attend your wedding rehearsal. I wouldn't miss it."

"Seriously, Jason. I'm not trying to be crass here, but I don't want your vice getting in the way this weekend. Have a nooner or something. Just don't miss it."

"I can go a day without having sex, Laina. I won't explode or anything. I did it when I was staying with Monty. Almost two weeks in a row actually."

There was a long pause on the other end of the line.

"Are you still there?" Jason asked.

"Yeah. I know you can do it, but maybe this weekend isn't the time to try. I need you sharp."

"Why? I'm not the one getting married."

She sighed. "No, but… I need you vigilant in case something happens. Silas was going to talk to you about this."

"Spill it." His older brother, Silas, wasn't exactly chatty these days. If he had something to talk to Jason about, it was most certainly bad news.

"He put the word out about Alex and Nickelova to Soleil and the other celestial fae at Maison des Étoilles."

Maison des Étoilles or Mansion of the Stars was a bordello owned and run by celestial fae—supernatural beings that drew their powers from heavenly bodies. The madam, Soleil, was an ex-girlfriend of Silas's. True to her name, Soleil's anchor of power was the sun, a boon for Silas as her presence could delay his need to shift. They'd broken up recently, but the two had remained friends, which was helpful to Jason's detective brother because the bordello tended to serve the underbelly of the city. The girls knew things, and lucky for Silas, were willing to talk.

"That's old news, sister. He asked her for help months ago. Last I heard, there'd been no sign of Nickelova or of Alex since you ripped through his abdomen," Jason said.

"There wasn't. Until now."

"What's happened?" He pushed his laptop away to make room for his elbows, using one hand to massage the base of his aching skull. He'd had enough of the anxiety roller coaster but there was no getting off of this ride, not until Alex and Nickelova were dead.

"Someone broke into the vault at Bojingles Fae Hospital and stole fire lily juice. There was nothing on any of the internal security recordings, but when the invisible thief was leaving the hospital, a device outside the entrance caught her moonlit reflection in the glass door to the building. A specialist on Silas's team blew it up and refined the image. It was Nickelova."

"Fire lily juice?" The juice of the fire lily could only be collected and administered by the fae, but it could cure a wide range of injuries and illnesses in supernatural beings. "She's still trying to heal Alex."

"That's what Silas thinks too," Laina said. "I nearly bit Alex's abdomen in two. He was bleeding out. I have no idea how she's kept him alive so long, but what else would she be doing with it?"

"Does Silas have any idea where she is now?"

"That's where Soleil comes in. One of her patrons was asking around about supernatural healers last night. Could be a coincidence, but…"

"It could be someone helping her," he finished.

"We all know if she is anywhere near Carlton City, she'll target my wedding. Pack security is on high alert. And if she succeeds in healing Alex, the entire pack is at risk."

He licked his lips. "I'll be there and I'll make sure I'm ready for anything."

Once they said their good-byes, Jason walked the periphery of his condo, ensuring every door and window was locked. Nickelova was one fish he hoped would get away for good. Far, far away. He hadn't known she was a dragon fae when he slept with her. Hell, he hadn't known her at all. They'd met at a bar and he'd forgotten her first name almost immediately after they screwed. But she played him for a fool. She'd been helping Fireborn pack's deadliest enemy, Alex Ravien Bloodright, a rogue wolf whose goal was to kill Silas and gain control of the Lycanthropic Society. Nickelova had used Jason for information, to lure Silas out of hiding.

Jason rubbed his chest, a wave of guilt dragging him under again. He should have been more careful. He should have known Nickelova was supernatural. His vice had almost been his pack's undoing.

He finished off the bottle of wine, too antsy to work, and only flopped onto his bed when the hour and the alcohol got the best of him. "A service to the pack," he mumbled as he drifted off. "The cursed prince." He fell asleep, fully clothed, the empty wine bottle still in his hand.

TWO

The blissful nothingness of sleep was something Jason only appreciated when it was gone, shattered by the blare of his phone's ringtone. He forced one eye open, blinking rapidly against the lure of sleep. 4:30 a.m. Who the hell was ringing him at this hour?

His hand slapped clumsily at the phone, knocking the empty wine bottle he'd been sleeping with to the floor. It made a hollow sound as it rolled across the hardwood and clinked into the wall. Heavy with sleep paralysis, he fumbled with the device, desperate to stop the ringing. Somehow he managed to tap the screen and manipulate it close enough to his ear to be effective.

"Mr. Flynn? It's the night doorman. I have a Teresa in the lobby for you."

Teresa. Who the hell was Teresa? "Uh, who?"

"Redhead," the doorman whispered.

"Oh. From the gatehouse. Send her up."

Jason rolled out of bed and visited the bathroom for some last minute primping. He ran his fingers through his dark hair, swished some mouthwash to combat morning breath, and dripped Visine into his green eyes to get the red out. Two spritzes of an enchanted cologne he'd brought back from Monaco and he was ready for action. The witch who'd made it for him said it enhanced attraction. By all accounts, based on previous experience, he'd gotten what he paid for.

When the knock came, he was already at the door. She was still wearing her Bachman Building uniform, her smile taking up more than its share of real estate on her face. He invited her in and offered her a drink.

"Wine," she said. "Whatever you have that's good."

"Make yourself at home." He drifted to the bar, leaving her standing awkwardly in the center of the room. He'd finished off the white wine. He selected a bottle of red, Pinot Noir, and reached for the corkscrew.

"Do you live here full-time?" Teresa asked, staring at the oatmeal couch, lips parted slightly.

He was surprised by the question. "Last time I checked. Why?"

She turned in a circle. "But, I mean, um, did you move in recently?"

Oh, she was commenting on the décor or lack of it. "Warm minimalism," he said. He finished pouring and handed her the glass of red wine.

"Huh?"

"The design. Clean lines. Simple décor. It's supposed to make you feel like you are the most important and interesting thing in the room." He sipped his own wine. "I think it's working. You're clearly the most beautiful thing within these walls."

Her lips twitched, a blush creeping from beneath her collar. "Thank you."

"Come, darling, sit. You've been on your feet all night." He lowered himself onto the sofa and held out his hand. She glanced from her glass to the furniture, seemingly uncomfortable with drinking red wine on white upholstery. She abandoned the drink on the mantle and joined him, perching on the edge of the middle cushion.

"I never do this. I'm probably breaking some kind of rule coming up here," she said.

"No one in this building will say a word to you. I'll see to that." With nothing but empathy in his eyes, he rested an ankle on one knee, calculating how long he'd have to play with the mouse before the wolf could have his meal. "Now, tell me about yourself. What's an exquisite creature such as you doing working in the gatehouse? It doesn't take a genius to see you're overqualified for the position."

She paused for a moment, lips parted, eyes staring as if she'd been frozen in place.

"Teresa? Are you all right?" He rested a hand on her shoulder.

She buried her face in her hands.

"Teresa?"

The girl raised her head and all kinds of freaky hit the walls. Her eyes were white. Solid white and glowing like 60-watt incandescents.

"What the fuck?"

"Don't concern yourself, Jay, or should I call you Jason? It's so hard to know what's appropriate. You've had so many identities."

He'd know that voice anywhere. Lowering his chin, he narrowed his eyes at Teresa's possessed body. "Nickelova?"

"Call me Nickie." Teresa's head rotated on her neck, listing back and around while the redhead's features changed, morphing into those of a svelte woman with a sleek platinum bob. A wicked smile broke out across full red lips. "Miss me?"

"What are you doing here?" The words came out in an anxious slur.

She leaned toward him, catching the glass of wine as it fell from his shaking hand and placing it on the coffee table. Her face came close enough to his that he could feel her breath on his lips.

Although he pressed into the back of the couch in an effort to put distance between them, his body reacted to her nearness. He remembered how she looked, spread out before him on the bed or riding his cock like a jockey. He'd had her so many ways before discovering who or what she was and he'd loved every single second of it. Sex with Nickie was like shooting heroin; it went straight to your pleasure center. Magically delicious.

"Is this for me?" she asked, palming him through his jeans.

"Don't touch me." He swallowed, hard. "I should kill you after what you did to us."

"But you won't." She shrugged. "And just so you know, even if you did you'd be murdering the redhead whose body I'm possessing, not me." She snorted. "Besides, *I* didn't do anything to your family. That was Alex." She massaged him through his pants, cupping and sliding her hand in a way that sent electric pulses of pleasure through his body.

He wanted to stop her. She *repulsed* him. But his vice needed to be fed, and Nickie understood just how to administer the dose of medicine he needed. It was all he could do not to touch her, not to invite more of what she was handing out. There was no way he could force himself to push her away.

"Why are you here?" Jason murmured.

"We had something, Jason. Don't deny it. You felt our connection. You feel it now." She unzipped his pants and palmed his cock.

"Stop," he murmured.

"I need your help. Alex can no longer follow through on his end of the bargain. But you and I together? We'd be unstoppable. You could do what Alex couldn't. I need you to join me."

"No."

She stroked him harder. "The supernatural community has spent far too long denying who they are. With common leadership, a wolf and a dragon as king and queen, we could change everything. We wouldn't have to tiptoe around humans anymore. We'd be free."

"Do you hear how crazy that sounds? The supernatural communities have different traditions, different needs. They need different leaders. Plus, it's the law of the goddess that we don't interfere with humans." Jason was sweating now, leaning back against the couch as she worked his cock. He should push her away. He should run for his bedroom, lock himself inside. But he couldn't. His vice held the keys and was the only one driving.

"That's how things are, but if we work together, it can be different. We can make it better."

He groaned as her hands twisted and tugged in perfect rhythm. Teetering on the edge of an orgasm, Jason suppressed the self-loathing that threatened to dull the edge. He went emotionally numb, thrusting rhythmically against her hands. He needed this. He'd consider the consequences later.

"Remember," she whispered in his ear as she worked his cock. A map appeared in his mind, unraveling like a flag. There was a road, a river, and a space between two mountains. He didn't recognize the place but a feeling accompanied the planted thought. A feeling that he could find the location if he tried. "Come to me, Jason. I'll give you more of this. All that you can handle. Deny me, and pay the price."

For some reason, he opened his eyes, although the last thing he wanted was to see what was happening. On the contrary, he wanted to hide from reality, pretend it was someone else between his legs. But she met his gaze as she lowered her head to wrap her lips around him. That's when the wolf took over. Jason grabbed the sides of Nickie's head and fucked her mouth in earnest, pounding the back of her throat until his orgasm sent pulsing shocks that kicked through his body again and again. He tipped his head back, groaning at the ceiling.

When his wolf finally receded, his self-loathing was enough to make him pull away like he'd been burned, tears welling in his eyes.

Her lips peeled back from her teeth. "Oh, don't bother pulling away now, Jason. The deed's been done. You just signed a contract with your body, activated a curse—a little something to remember me by. From this day forward, every time you have sex, the act will bind you to me. It will give me power over you. I've planted how to find me in your brain. Don't try to tell anyone else; it won't work out well for you. You can either come to me of your own free will or wait until your vice makes you my robot. Either way, I'll see you soon."

"No. No, Nickie, don't do this."

But Nickie was gone. The redhead was back, on her knees in front of his crotch, looking utterly disgusted with herself.

Jason shivered and collected himself, the practiced smile snapping back into place. "Teresa," he drawled. "I can honestly say this has been a first for me." He tucked, straightened, and zipped.

The girl looked confused. She glanced at her drink as if he might have drugged her, but it was across the room where she'd left it on the mantle. She'd never even taken a sip.

"Thank you for a wonderful evening, er, morning." He helped her from the floor. "I'd love to make a day of it, but I have work. You understand."

She nodded slowly, stopping halfway to the door. "What happened? I can't remember."

He paused and took her hand. "Just two people taking solace from an unforgiving world in the safety of each other's arms. We broke through the daily loneliness, darling, connected on a spiritual level. I admit, I didn't think we were ready to take this step, but you were so insistent."

Even though he felt like an accomplice to a crime, he opened the door and showed her out. "I'll call you."

She smiled and gave him a half wave. "Bye."

As he closed the door, a soul-shaking tremble rumbled from deep within him. He staggered to the shower and turned the water on as hot as it would go. The soap wasn't strong enough but it would have to do. He scrubbed in the scalding heat, enduring the self-inflicted punishment he deserved.

He needed help. But who could he trust? If he told Silas about what happened, he might find himself without a head. Or, more likely, without a pack. But if he told no one, Nickie would use his vice to make him her slave. Because even as he struggled to wash all remnants of her from his body, a tiny voice inside his head was already whispering about how much he'd enjoyed her and how incredible it would be to have her again.

THREE

Jason arrived in Red Grove that night feeling twitchy and uneasy. It didn't help that the tiny town was home to a cemetery that stretched on for miles, the army of headstones ending at the creepy Victorian home of demigoddess witch, Grateful Knight. No way did he want to run into her or her caretaker husband. The witch was a friend of Silas's, but Jason always found her eerily unsettling.

Per Laina's instructions, he turned down a winding road that led deep into the woods and parked near the quaint cabin by the lake where Kyle and Laina now lived. He could see why his sister wanted to get married here; the place was untarnished and magical. The early spring blossoms on the trees above shed petals that swirled overhead and weighed the air with a fantastical whimsy.

"Welcome. You must be Jason," a melodious voice said. He scented her before he saw her, his wolf nose detecting a luscious concoction of mango and vanilla with a hint of spice on the breeze. When he divined the source, he was not disappointed. She was tall, willowy, and dressed in a flowing pink robe that matched the blush of the petals that circled her perfectly coifed caramel-colored hair. Standing beside the twisting branches of an oak tree, she smiled at him, and the effect was like something out of a dream. Jason's wolf responded so fast and hard his legs stopped working. He froze, staring at her dumbly.

"Are you all right?" she asked, rushing forward to take his arm.

Her eyes were violet, a rare color he thought must actually be blue in the right light. But it was the innocence in those eyes and the soft, graceful way she touched his shoulder that unsettled him the most. His usually suave and practiced demeanor was nowhere to be found. He struggled to find his voice.

"I'm here for the rehearsal," Jason said quietly.

The woman nodded. "Of course you are." Removing one of the white flower leis that hung from the nook of her elbow, she lowered it around his neck. "I'm Selene. I'm an acolyte working with Artemis on your sister's wedding. I don't believe we've ever formally met."

"No," he said. He would have remembered meeting her. For forever and a day.

"I'm honored to help today. I'll show you back to where the others are waiting and where the ceremony will take place tomorrow.

"Am I late?" he asked.

"No. We are still waiting for the groom's brother to arrive."

Thank the goddess.

"Wait… Did you say you're an acolyte?" he asked. "You're pursuing the werewolf priesthood?" Jason's face tightened and he realized too late that he was making a face like he'd smelled something bad. Her eyebrows drew together and her gaze dropped to the forest floor.

"Yes," she said curtly. "If you'll follow me, the others are this way." She pointed a hand toward a trail leading into the trees. He followed her, walking side by side on the narrow path in silence. Had he offended her?

"I'm sorry for the reaction," Jason finally said. "To you being an acolyte. That was rude of me. I haven't been myself today. This is all… harder than I expected." Goddess, he wanted to pull the bow at her waist and slip that robe off her shoulders. He furtively watched the silk tug against her nipple as she walked.

"It's normal to feel some anxiety about your sister getting married. You may have feelings of pressure to marry yourself or fear that you will never find a mate."

No, Jason thought, *neither of those things.*

"Think of it like this, you're not losing a sister, you're gaining a brother," she continued. "The scrolls say that a wedding of any within the pack is a reminder of our unity as a species. We are stronger when we work as one."

Her words hit him like a bucket of ice water. "The scrolls?" He laughed cynically.

"You're not a fan of our holy texts?"

"No offense, but I find it hard to believe that a goddess loved wolves so much that she turned twelve of them into men, only to curse them to return to their true form for three nights a month during the full moon. Oh, and while she was at it, further cursed them with individual vices that rule their lives almost as much as the turning into an animal once a month thing does." He laughed acerbically. "If there is truly a goddess, she's a bitch."

Selene balked, her jaw dropping. "The goddess did not curse us," she said. "It was a blessing. She allowed us to retain an echo of our animal selves while inheriting a higher consciousness. Unlike our animal ancestors, werewolves have free will—we can choose. Our Primary ancestors were as close to wolves as humans have ever been and powerful enough to birth our entire race."

Jason snorted. Why were all the beautiful ones crazy? "Or a Homo sapien got it on with a wolf and we evolved. Seems more likely."

"Why would that be more likely?"

Because I don't feel like a person with higher consciousness or free will, he thought. *I feel like an exhausted werewolf orphan who has to live a lie just to survive.* "I just don't believe the scrolls are anything more than stories. They're fiction."

Long tapered fingers landed on Jason's forearm and he paused to look at her. "It is clear to me you are struggling with a deeply spiritual issue at this moment," she said. "I will pray for you, Jason Flynn, and light a candle for you in our sanctuary. If you wish to heal this thing within yourself, please come see us. That's what the *Preotka* and her acolytes are for. We help when you can't figure things out on your own."

Jason tried to disguise his scowl. It was well known that the *Preotka* and her acolytes lived a celibate lifestyle in an effort to enhance their spiritual connection with the next world. Even now, Selene's expression held not a flicker of cynicism or doubt. She looked at him like he was the only person on this earth and the purpose of her entire existence was to genuinely help him. *Fuck.* How could he ever accept her help, knowing that if he shared his vice, shared about the things he'd done and wanted to do… he'd be ruining her innocence, tainting the very soul who so generously wanted to help him.

He grazed his bottom lip along his upper teeth. "I don't think what's broken inside me can be fixed."

"*Preotka* Artemis says that brokenness is the first step toward transformation. A caterpillar completely takes itself apart in order to become a butterfly."

"Gotta break a few eggs to make an omelet, eh?"

"She doesn't mean—"

He held up a hand. "Save your breath. My egg was fried on the sidewalk a long time ago. The only transformation happening here"—he placed a hand on his gut and winked—"is happening to the burger I had for lunch."

She pressed two fingers to her lips, covering a hint of a smile. They'd arrived at the clearing where Laina, Kyle, and Silas were waiting for him.

"Well, just think about it," Selene said. "It would be my pleasure to work with you. My door is always open."

As he watched Selene drift away, Jason wished he could take advantage of her open door, and not in the religious way. The thought confirmed he was a filthy predator. He sighed. Every moment with Selene would be like looking at his dark soul under a magnifying glass. She was pure, unadulterated virtue. A person like that could make anyone feel unworthy.

* * * * *

Selene watched Jason cross to his siblings with mild fascination. It wasn't every day a person got this close to the royal family. Oh, she'd been in Jason's presence before at pack events and during the shift, although they'd never been formally introduced. It wasn't odd for a royal to overlook a simple acolyte. But she'd never fully appreciated the rumors until now. He was strikingly handsome up close; her stomach had done an odd little twist when he'd looked at her. And he was charming. Witty. Someone she imagined one could talk to all day without growing weary. Although she detected a darkness in his soul she wasn't expecting, a darkness she found more disturbing by the minute.

"What were you talking to Prince Jason about?" Artemis asked, her soft and straightforward smile giving her a younger appearance than her wrinkled skin and gray curls would suggest. She clasped her hands beneath the bell sleeves of her heavy purple robe.

"I sense something is troubling Jason, *Preotka*. He has a deep unease about him this day. I suggested it was common for a brother to feel anxious over a sibling's marriage, but his words seemed to indicate the problem goes deeper." She shook her head.

"And his aura?" Artemis was testing her. Aura reading was *Preotka* magic, something Selene was learning but hadn't fully mastered, like everything else in her chosen vocation.

"Muddy, with a green center. Much darker than it should be." She tangled her fingers beneath the sleeves of her robe, nervous about the accuracy of her reading.

"I fear you are correct, sister. Are you aware of Jason's vice?"

Selene shook her head. She understood that some wolves had vices, intense addictions to things or people that grew stronger near the full moon, but they tended to be relatively harmless and easily fulfilled. Caffeine addiction was common or an increased need for raw meat. Vices were private annoyances, not something most wolves talked about openly.

"His vice is sex."

Heat flushed Selene's face and she placed her fingers on her warm cheeks in surprise. "But he's not mated," she whispered.

Artemis shook her head. "He has sex with many different women at all times of the month to feed his addiction, and I've recently heard his need is getting worse."

"But that's dangerous. Aside from the risk of unintended pregnancies, what must it do to his soul to connect intimately with so many people?" Thank the goddess that werewolves were immune to sexually transmitted infections and couldn't catch or transmit human diseases. She shivered to think of the risk he'd be taking if they weren't.

Artemis nodded her head slowly. "I have seen this before."

"You have?"

"This isn't a simple vice, Selene. Jason's human side is addicted as well. It started with the wolf but I fear the addiction has afflicted the man."

"What did you do when you saw this before?"

"Breaking a vice requires intensive spiritual therapy. Only about half of these cases ever recover. Some die."

Selene inhaled sharply. "Do you think the prince could die of his vice?"

"Shhh." Artemis raised a finger to her lips. "They'll hear you."

"Forgive me." Selene composed herself, folding her hands in front of her hips and bowing her head.

"I believe this vice will destroy Jason—if not physically, then emotionally—unless he gains control soon. This need of his has become a dragon. If he continues feeding it, the beast will eat him alive." Artemis gave Selene a knowing smile.

"How can you tell, *Preotka*?"

The old woman's rheumy gaze drifted toward the royal family. "Experience. I've seen it before, with others."

"There must be something we can do."

"Vices have been overcome before with help from the goddess. But he must *want* to be free of his addiction. He must choose a new path."

Selene glanced over her shoulder at the group of royals gathered near the makeshift altar. Gerty and her husband Arthur, the king and queen of the woodland fae who called this forest home, had emerged from their trees and were mingling with the rest of the wedding party. Nate, the groom's brother, had also arrived. It was time to begin the rehearsal.

Quickly, Selene said, "Perhaps if I spoke to him, let him know we are willing to help and that he has the power to break the spell this vice has over him?"

"You have my permission to try, Selene. If you succeed, with help from the goddess, I will seriously consider it a sign you are fit for the next level on your spiritual journey." Artemis kissed her forehead and drifted toward the others.

A swell of pride filled Selene. The next phase of her spiritual journey was to advance to *Preotka*, to become priestess. It was the goal of every acolyte to be promoted to priestess and devote her life to serving the spiritual needs of the pack, but most acolytes never made it. Could she be one of the rare exceptions? A werewolf acolyte strong enough to win the goddess's favor and advance to the most respected role in the priesthood?

All that stood in her way of achieving the pinnacle of her life's work was Jason Flynn and his vice.

FOUR

Jason checked his watch for the third time in fifteen minutes. He loved his sister, but the crawling sensation under his skin was only getting worse. After the incident with Nickelova that morning, his vice should have been appeased for at least twenty-four hours, but the release proved superficial. His wolf was already begging for more, his need like a spring coiled too tight, ready to snap. He pumped his leg and wished Artemis would talk faster.

"Jason, I want you to carry the gifts for the goddess in the processional." Laina pointed at a prop platter with plastic fruit.

"Huh?" A bead of sweat narrowly missed his left eye, prompting a swipe of the back of his hand across his forehead.

"Silas is walking me down the aisle. I thought this would be a good way to involve you in the ceremony."

With a tight smile, he picked up the tray, blinking rapidly. "Of course. I… I'm happy to." Surely he could carry a platter of fruit? He licked his lips, his mouth as dry as the Sahara.

After a nod of appreciation in Jason's direction, *Preotka* Artemis began walking them through the ceremony from start to finish. She took extra time with Kyle and his brother Nate since their human upbringing meant they were unfamiliar with pack traditions. Night was upon them, the half-moon bathing the venue in a subtle glow. When Laina and Kyle were in position, practicing their vows, Gerty waved her wand in the air and sent a legion of fireflies to light up the space above their heads. Everyone oohed and ahhed at the display.

Jason tried to appreciate the beauty around him, but he couldn't. His hands trembled beneath the tray of fake fruit. He was sweating in earnest now. At the first opportunity, he set the offering down and removed his leather jacket, despite it being a cool spring day.

"What's the matter with you?" Silas whispered. "You're sweating like a wiener on a Fourth of July grill."

Jason ran a finger along the inside of his collar. "Feeling a little under the weather. I need a drink."

"Did you… feed the wolf?"

"This morning." It wasn't a lie. No need to tell him about Nickelova.

Silas frowned. "It's getting worse."

"Like a bad flu."

"How did this happen? You've had this under control for years."

"Hell if I know." The lie was quick and firm, his eyes focused on the altar to make it harder for Silas to detect. Running a hand over his face, Jason decided to do something he never thought he would do. "Can you alpha this out of me, Silas?" He gave his brother a tired laugh. "You know, take the edge off."

"That bad, eh?" Silas rubbed the stubble of his chin and contemplated his brother in silence. "I wish it were that easy. When Laina discovered her need for Kyle, I researched breaking a vice with an alpha command." Silas grimaced. "If history is to be believed, it wouldn't end well. With a vice like yours, you might not be capable of obeying me. You'd likely do it anyway. The result would be painful, a perpetual hell where you increasingly wanted sex but couldn't have it without pain. It would drive you insane."

"Sounds unpleasant." Jason rubbed the base of his skull. His headache was back with a vengeance.

"There is a way to break a vice, though. I read about it in the same texts."

"Yeah? How?"

Silas pointed his chin toward the gray-haired woman reviewing the ceremony at the front of the aisle.

"Artemis?" Jason scoffed. "Yes, I'm sure a celibate woman twice my age will have helpful tips on how I can wrestle my sexual vice under control."

"She's not just a priestess in name. She and her followers have gifts from the goddess. A little of her voodoo would do you good, give you the advantage to break the hold this vice has over you."

"I can't think of anything more humiliating than talking to the priestess about this."

A burly palm slapped his shoulder and shook gently. "She knows, Jason. Everyone knows."

Jason narrowed his eyes. "I stand corrected. Knowing she knows is far more humiliating. Do you talk about my vice over coffee?"

"No. No one had to tell her outright. You've been with half the pack, brother. Word gets around."

With a deep breath, Jason glanced toward Artemis, but it was the acolyte, Selene, standing behind her that commanded his attention. Dressed in that elegant blush-colored robe, she stared at him as if he were a puzzle she wished to solve. More accurately, she stared through him. *She knew*, he realized. Those violet, self-righteous eyes cut right through him, no doubt analyzing his soul.

"Just think about it," Silas said.

Jason stared at Selene, picturing her naked and tied spread-eagle to his bed. He wondered if her sex was the same petal pink as her robe. No, Artemis couldn't help him and neither could Selene. Hell, the way his wolf was eyeing her as his next meal, he'd be wise to stay as far away from her as possible.

* * *

Why is he staring at me? Selene locked eyes with Jason. The look on the man's face was that of a drowning man. Indeed, the intensity of his stare made her uncomfortable, stirred something deep inside her she hadn't known was there. Her heart rate increased, its thump steady in her ears, and a tingle started deep within her abdomen. *Deep empathy,* she thought. A level of compassion she'd never achieved before. With a start, she recognized it must be the goddess calling her to help this man. The strong swelling in her chest was a sign from above.

But could she do it? Although she'd been trained to treat addictions in general, she knew little about sex. Plus, she'd never put what few skills she had to use before. Not because she didn't want to, of course. It was simply that an opportunity hadn't presented itself.

Jason was obviously uncomfortable. Even from a distance, his face looked flushed and his hands trembled by his sides. His brother and pack alpha, Silas, seemed genuinely concerned. If she could convince Jason to let her help him, not only would she save a member of the royal family from the pain she sensed he was in, but she could ease an obviously strained familial relationship.

Helping Jason was her first priority, but in the back of her mind, she also felt an urgent need to prove to Artemis she was right for the priesthood. She must talk to him, must convince him to let her help.

"I believe that covers everything," Artemis announced from the altar in front of her. "I'll see you all back here tomorrow for the real thing."

As the wedding party broke up and a swell of chatting signaled the happy couple's departure from the altar, Selene drifted toward Jason, hoping for another chance to convince him to work with her. But when she reached the place where he'd been standing with his brother, he was gone.

FIVE

Jason rushed from the wedding rehearsal feeling like he had a bad case of poison ivy. His skin itched and burned, and the throb at the base of his skull had grown more intense. *Boom, boom, boom.* The pain demanded attention.

He reached into his glove compartment and fished out a bottle of pain relievers, popping the cap and dry-swallowing three. The pounding took on a rhythm, morphing into a voice, Nickelova's voice. *Come to me. Come to me.* Her command echoed in his head until it became a stabbing sensation. He rubbed where it hurt the most. Jason had a nagging suspicion the discomfort was only going to get worse unless he found a way to break the curse. He needed help—magic powerful enough to undo what Nickelova had done to him. And he had an idea where he might find it.

Exiting the highway deep within Carlton City, Jason drove down the alley behind the Mill Wheel Night Club, wishing he'd had the forethought to bring a gun loaded with wooden bullets. A couple making out behind a dumpster turned their heads long enough for the two puncture wounds on the woman's neck to gurgle blood that ran in lazy rivulets into her cleavage. Fuck, he hated vamps. If he wasn't desperate for a solution to his Nickelova problem, he'd never risk this part of town.

He parked under a rectangular tin sign that read *Ryker's Lost Things*. The logo was a chipped etching of a boy with a handkerchief on a stick over his shoulder, an unsettling smile on his freckled face. The sign squeaked on rusty hinges as it swung in the evening breeze.

Jason had loaned Ryker his start-up capital for this place, despite shady references and a business plan that was one step up from a cocktail napkin. Only Ryker proved persuasive, so persuasive that Jason caught on quickly that his aptitude for business wasn't quite human. And based on the return he'd seen come through his e-mail, the guy had serious connections inside the world of the occult.

The bell over the door chimed and the smell of dust hit Jason's nostrils. The inside of Lost Things looked like an episode of hoarders. Stacks of books, artifacts, and shiny objects crowded the doorway. He had to turn sideways to slip between two large crates of Fabergé eggs, pausing halfway through when a low hum met his superhuman ears. It emanated from one large black egg that gleamed in the dim light, its ebony luster drawing him in. He leaned over for a better look.

"Don't touch that," came a smooth voice from deep within the shop. "Unless you'd like to spend the night locked inside that shiny trinket. I won't be able to get you out until sunrise. I need to move them into the back room. Haven't had a chance."

Jason stepped back from the eggs and made his way deeper into the dimly lit store. A squat woman waddled up to the counter with a handful of dried lizards. Her T-shirt read, *Witches do it in circles.*

"Do you sell these in bulk?" she asked the dark man behind the counter.

"Five for twenty."

The woman plopped down a bill. She waddled out the door, giving a wide clearance to the crate of eggs.

"Ryker Vandoren, how's my favorite client?" Jason spread his arms wide.

The man glanced up from his work and promptly disappeared, becoming a twist of smoke in a blink of an eye. The dark fog rolled over the counter and through the hodgepodge of collectibles. Ryker rematerialized near Jason, smelling of sulfur and dried things. Black eyes burned above a smile that boasted two overdeveloped cuspids. His olive-toned skin seemed to give off its own light in the haze of dust around them.

"Favorite client?" he asked. "Never try to charm an incubus, Mr. Flynn." His voice was pure silk and flowed from full lips like a whispered seduction. "It makes you seem insincere."

"Call me Jason. I assure you, I'd never attempt to charm you, Ryker. It would be like trying to sell an air conditioner to a polar bear."

Ryker blinked upturned eyes, a ghost of a smile turning the corners of his mouth. He narrowed his gaze on Jason. "What brings you here today? I've honored our agreement. Are you unhappy with your rate of return?"

"On the contrary, I'm impressed with your success. Who knew an antique shop for magical artifacts would do so well in the vampire district?" He rubbed the ache at the back of his head. "No, I'm not here about my investment."

The demon gestured toward the store. "Then what can I do for you?"

"I have a problem, and I think you might have a solution. But I need you to promise to keep this confidential."

Ryker's ears bent forward slightly. "We are alone. Your secrets are safe with me. I assure you, I have many."

"Well, yes. I assumed. That's why I came to you. I need your help. I have a problem with a dragon fae."

With a step back and a hiss, Ryker shook his finger. "Dragon fae are not my area of expertise. If you've offended the female, I suggest you apologize."

"How did you know I was talking about a female?"

"Because the only dragon fae to be in this city in a century is female."

"You've seen her?"

"No. But I've heard."

"I had a relationship with her."

"A physical relationship?"

Jason lowered his chin and gave an almost imperceptible nod. "And now she's haunting me."

The incubus's long tapered fingers lifted to his mouth to conceal a chuckle. "Even *I* wouldn't risk an affair with a dragon." Ryker's barbed tail twitched behind him.

"For your information, I didn't know she was fae when I was, er, drinking from her teacup. And now she's possessing women I'm with and saying that every time I have sex I'll trigger some kind of curse that will make me her slave."

The demon inhaled through his teeth.

"I need a way to break her curse."

Ryker took another deep breath and let it out slowly. "The only way to break the curse of a dragon is to remove her heart."

"As much as I'd like to do that, first I'd have to find her, and then I'd have to have a plan for removing said heart. That might take a while. In the meantime, you must have a talisman or an enchanted gem that will disconnect her from my... business?"

The laugh Ryker let out was gritty as though his throat was lined with hot coals. "I am not a doctor or a witch... or a witch doctor, for that matter." He quirked an eyebrow. "I'm a demon, an incubus to be exact. I don't know for sure the nature of this dragon's curse. Only another fae would know for sure. But the fact that she possessed a woman you were with and didn't simply pop into your bedroom does tell us something."

"Like what?"

"Like there's probably a reason she can't come to you physically," he said. "She's cursed you to come to her because she can't come to you. That's likely why she used your vice." Although Ryker used a matter-of-fact tone when he said the word "vice," Jason scowled. "You didn't think I was aware of your vice? I feed off sexual energy, Jason. I smelled it on you the moment we met. Your reputation filled in the gaps. My presumption is, when you had sex with the dragon fae, she cursed your vice."

"Just my vice?"

Ryker pointed at Jason's cell phone poking from his suit pocket. "From what I've been told, a dragon's curse can act like a virus someone e-mailed to you. Every time you click on the link it runs a program that accomplishes something nefarious in your device.

Magic can attach to things, be introduced to a host in various ways. You are both man and beast but your vice is the lowest common denominator between the two. The dragon fae left you a gift where it counts. Every time you get busy, she gets busy. A curse like that could be used to track your whereabouts, visit you through the body of your partner, influence your mind, even mess with your chemistry. All from the comfort of whatever hole she's hiding in."

"Mess with my chemistry?"

"Have you noticed your vice growing stronger? Harder to manage? You've got a monkey on your back for sex, my friend, and I'm willing to bet that monkey is about to get much heavier."

"So she makes my vice worse but every time I indulge it, the curse brings me closer to being her robot."

"Exactly."

"Fucking fantastic." Jason took a deep breath. "You need to help me. You have magical objects from every corner of the earth in here. There must be something that can extract a dragon fae curse."

He rubbed the smooth skin of his chin. There was a rumor that incubus demons were completely hairless aside from their eyebrows and the tops of their heads. Jason tried not to think too much about it or about how the man survived as an incubus.

"There is something…" Ryker said, eyes darting around the shop.

"Please."

"I have procured a demonic object with promising capabilities, but there is no record of a werewolf ever using it. Your kind is more human than my kind. There could be side effects."

"Tell me more."

Ryker coupled his hands behind his back and made his way through the stacks toward the office door behind the counter. He fished something out of a case on the desk.

"Once there was a demon who fell in love with a human. She wanted exclusivity. Silly. My kind is incapable of monogamy. But the desperate demon commissioned this from a witch." He held out a box with a carving of a serpent eating its own tail on the lid.

Jason flipped the box open, revealing a shiny platinum snake, body straight as a pin. "What does it do?"

"It mutates sexual desire into another form. For this male, sex became hunger. It worked for a while. He took sexual nourishment only from his mate and filled his lust for others with food."

Jason reached for the box. "So then why is it here and not on some incubus living happily ever after?"

"The female left him. The demon, in his grief, refused to take off the ring. He ate himself to death. At least that's the rumor. I can't be responsible for verifying the stories of every treasure in this place."

"But if I wear this, I can avoid having sex. And if I avoid having sex, I avoid Nickelova."

"Nickelova! You *are* in deep. I was not aware it was the princess of the Siberian dragon fae who was gracing us with her presence."

Jason sighed. "How much for the ring?"

"You'd do better to visit a witch familiar with your kind. This might not be safe for you."

"How much?"

The demon considered him for a moment. "Forgiveness of my remaining debt to you should do it."

Pausing for a moment, Jason did a quick calculation in his head. It wasn't much by his standards, and the royalties on his investment far exceeded the investment itself. "Only relief of debt. No change in ownership percentage."

Ryker bowed his head slightly in agreement.

"How do I use it?"

"Put it on your finger."

Instead of asking how he was supposed to wear a straight piece of jewelry like a ring, Jason poked the silver serpent. The snake came alive, inched over his knuckle, and coiled itself around his pointer finger. Immediately, the dull ache he constantly carried between his legs eased. Or maybe it just changed into something else. The heavy weight of sexual need was now a feeling of nausea, like he was in the first days of a stomach flu.

"I think it's working," he said.

"Good." Ryker narrowed his eyes at Jason, a cross between concern and self-preservation coming through his features. "As a precaution, don't leave it on all the time. Have you heard of Maison des Étoilles?"

Jason snorted. He knew Maison des Étoilles well. His brother, Silas, had dated the madam of the famed bordello. "I've heard of it."

"It's run by celestial fae. If there were a group as powerful as dragon fae, the celestial variety would be it. Not only are they resistant to another fae's possession, they have protections on the building that may prevent the activation of Nickelova's curse. Think of their magic as antivirus software." He pointed at Jason's phone again. "Go regularly. Take the ring off and feed your wolf."

"Thanks for the advice, but I've never had to pay for sex before and I don't intend to start now." He'd also rather not frequent a bordello run by his brother's ex—who still occasionally chatted with his big bro. The farther he could keep this problem from Silas and Laina the better.

Ryker shook his head. "Jason, about this ring…" He trailed off as if considering whether to share more.

"What about it?"

"It's a temporary fix. It stores up all the wanting, all the desire you feel while you wear it, and channels it into something else. But the moment you take it off, everything you were avoiding comes back exponentially stronger than before. Make sure you are in a safe place to vent your pent-up desires." Ryker handed him the wooden box the ring came in. "Also, keep it in this when you're not wearing it. Could be dangerous in the wrong hands. It's your responsibility now."

Jason accepted the box, a stiff sweat breaking out on his upper lip. "I think I need some air."

"Hmm." Ryker dissolved into a dark fog and blew through the store, reforming at the entrance to hold the door open for Jason.

Feeling feverish and more than a little woozy, Jason made his way through the stacks to meet Ryker at the exit. He stumbled toward his Bugatti.

"Oh, and Jason…"

"Yeah?"

"Are you fucking crazy driving that thing in this neighborhood? Count yourself lucky you still have four wheels."

With a two-fingered salute, Jason slid behind the wheel and headed for home.

SIX

The ring was working. Jason hadn't had a sexual encounter since Nickelova and was still semifunctional, thanks to the silver serpent. Unlike the ring's previous owner, Jason's sex drive hadn't channeled itself into hunger. On the contrary, he couldn't bring himself to eat a single thing. Instead, the enchanted object had caused a perpetual state of lethargy and periods of fever as if he were fighting off a human illness. But with twelve hours of sleep and the maximum allowable dose of pain medication, he felt almost normal as he proceeded down the aisle at his sister's wedding as planned, the offering to the goddess balanced on his palms.

Alight with fireflies, the forest brimmed with dancing woodland fae who sang from the branches of their trees. Flower petals spiraled through the night sky over their heads, to the delight of the guests who sat in white folding chairs on either side of the aisle. Jason set the offering on the altar and took his position to the side, next to the other groomsmen.

Laina made a beautiful bride. Her off-the-shoulder gossamer gown seemed to float around her as she strode down the aisle. A canopy of bright green branches blossomed with glittering fairy magic above her head. And when she reached Kyle, it was clear the groom only had eyes for her. His hands wrapped around hers, entangled fingers a physical symbol of the sacred vows they were about to recite. How lucky she was. It was a goddamned miracle to be loved, really loved, and to give love back to someone in return.

Once the vows were exchanged, Laina detached the specially designed sleeve of Kyle's tux for the tattooing ritual. The bicep-tricep combo on the guy was as big as Jason's head. If he didn't know better, he'd swear Kyle was a mature shifter, not a *dormant* as he was known to be. Clearly, his size and general appearance placed him in the more-than-human category.

Which made Jason even more aware of how less-than-werewolf he was at the moment. His normally muscular upper body had grown thin and wiry over the last few months. Not because of his vice per se, but because he never ate anymore. He couldn't remember the last time he sat down to three squares in a day unless you counted copious amounts of alcohol as a meal. And considering his increased metabolism—most wolves ate the equivalent of four humans—Jason's occasional cheeseburger was barely keeping him from starving to death.

Artemis pressed the fang of Fireborn pack's Primary ancestor to Kyle's right shoulder, carving the tribal phoenix tattoo that denoted their pack. It was said the magic of the artifact caused the actual staining of the skin, but Jason always assumed it was a trick: ink stored inside the hollow of the massive tooth. With that symbol on his shoulder, werewolf or not, he'd be one of them now, bound to protect and be protected by the pack. The *Preotka* shifted for a better angle and Jason's gaze fell on Selene.

His mouth bent into a grimace. Why did she vex him so? She was kind enough and beautiful… astonishingly beautiful. In any other scenario, he'd be trying to get her into his bed. Only Selene was fine china. Aside from her celibate role as a religious acolyte for the pack, everything about her was pure and delicate. Untainted. He was afraid to speak to her for fear his words might pollute her ears. When she looked at him, he was sure she could see every grain of filth he hid behind his expensive clothes and brash attitude. And the thought of touching her… If there were anything good left inside him, he'd never sully her with direct contact.

Once again she was staring at him. Probably judging him. Yep, he was the one addicted to sex.

With a sigh, he looked away, straight at the rows of guests. The witch, Grateful Knight, was in the second row with her husband, Rick, a young boy bouncing on his hip. That must be their son, Lucas. Cameron James was there too. Nice of him to come, given he'd been the one in the tux at the altar with Laina only a few months ago.

Why was this taking so long? The familiar crawling feeling had begun again, like an army of ants rushing beneath his epidermis. He scratched his wrist. A breeze rustled the trees overhead but he was melting inside his tux. Rocking onto his heels, he tugged at his collar.

Anxiously, he twisted the serpent ring on his finger and a wave of nausea came over him. Everyone was clapping. Why was everyone clapping? Oh, his sister. Artemis had announced the happy couple as officially married. Jason put his hands together in a delayed clap.

A buzz started in his ears, growing loud enough to drown everything else out. At first, it was white noise. Then the buzz took on a familiar rhythm, words he'd hoped had gone away came flooding back into his head. *Come to me. Come to me.* Nickelova's voice haunted him with every throb of his cranium. Louder and louder. It stabbed into his gray matter, constricting his vision.

Laina and Kyle walked down the aisle to whoops and howls of celebration. He was supposed to do something. Silas nudged his elbow and he realized he was supposed to follow. He fell into step, working his way up the aisle between the chairs.

The voice grew louder and faster. *Come to me. COME TO ME.* Jason pitched forward, grabbing his head as a lightning strike cut through his brain. He moaned.

"What's wrong? Jason? Jason!" Silas was by his side, but there was nothing his brother could do. The horizon tilted and his cheek slapped the white cotton runner. A woman screamed. Silas bent over him, shook his shoulder.

But Jason couldn't respond. All he could see was Nickelova's face. All he could hear was her voice. *Come to me.* And all he could see was a road, a river, and a space between two mountains. This time he recognized the road. Route 9. And that was the Stone Eagle River winding under it. He could go to her. It would be easier if he'd go.

His eyes rolled back in his head and his back arched off the soft cloth runner, and then, mercifully, there was nothing.

* * * * *

Selene reached Jason's fallen body about the same time everyone else did. At the back of the impenetrable crowd, she craned her ear in his direction for any information on his condition.

"His vitals are normal," Grateful Knight said. That's right, she was a nurse as well as a witch. "There's nothing physically wrong with him. This is something magical, Silas."

There was a swoosh and the crowd parted slightly, giving Selene a view of the witch and her glowing purple sword. Grateful Knight was no ordinary witch. She was a Hecate, a demigoddess with an immortal soul charged with policing the supernatural. Selene gasped as she lowered her weapon toward Jason's body, causing his skin to illuminate.

"When Nightshade touches him, he lights up like a lightbulb," Grateful said. "What the hell?" The tip of her sword glided down his arm, moving as if of its own volition. It stopped at his finger. Selene leaned forward to get a better look. The sword tip pointed at a serpent shaped ring. With a short jab, Nightshade's tip connected with the object.

An ear-piercing shriek emanated from the jewelry. The silver dropped from Jason's skin and inched away through the grass. Grateful raised her sword above her head and stabbed the silver serpent. With a shriek, the worm disappeared in a puff of smoke.

"What was that thing?" Silas asked.

"Whatever it was, it was enchanted with very dark magic." Grateful returned to Jason's unconscious body, the sword glowing to life again. "It isn't just the ring, although I'm sensing it was exasperating his condition. There's something inside him. It's like… It's almost as if…"

"He's been cursed," Gerty said.

"Yes, cursed." Grateful nodded. "Do you know who might have done this?"

"I do," Gerty said. She glanced at Silas, Laina, and Kyle, the last of whom was rubbing his new wife's shoulders in a way that seemed to be the only thing propping her up.

There was a long pause, followed by frantic whispering. Selene strained to hear, but the whispers drifted away on the spring breeze. Artemis stepped beside her, a look of supreme concern on her face.

"It appears you were correct about Prince Jason's aura," the older woman whispered. "There is more amiss than a simple vice."

She was interrupted when Silas spoke. "Let's move him somewhere safe. Somewhere we can assess him properly." The crowd parted and Silas hoisted Jason into his arms.

Laina placed a hand on her stomach, whispering something to Kyle over her shoulder. He nodded in agreement. "Bring him to the cabin. It's closest." There was an exchange of whispers between the royal family and Grateful Knight, and then all of them scattered.

Selene let out a deep breath and slumped her shoulders as the group disappeared into the woods, following the pathway back to the parking area.

Artemis cleared her throat. "It has been a long day, sister. I wonder if you might accompany the royal family and tend to their spiritual needs. I must rest."

"Yes," Selene said with enthusiasm. "I'd be happy to."

"Very well. Remember, the goddess is Jason's hope for recovery." Artemis handed her the box containing the Fireborn Primary Alpha artifacts, the same ones she'd used to bind Laina and Kyle just moments ago. Selene gazed at the sacred chest in wonder, honored to be trusted with it. Artemis graced her with a confident smile. "Break this curse, sister, then see if you can help the man."

SEVEN

"Artemis sent me. I'm here to help." Selene ignored the slight shake of her knees and raised her chin in an effort to convey competence.

To her relief, Princess Laina allowed her inside the small cottage and led her to the bedroom where Jason had been laid out atop the bed's patchwork quilt. The crowd she'd seen before had thinned considerably, with only Silas, Laina, and Gerty surrounding Jason in the small room. It was clear the royal family wanted to handle Jason's condition discretely.

"This is the work of dragon fae," Gerty said, smoothing her silver hair and lowering her chin to look at Silas over her bifocals. "Nickelova's magic, I'm sure of it. Dragon fae magic is rare and I fear, stronger than mine."

"Can you break the curse?" Silas asked.

Gerty approached Jason's body, drawing her wand. "Water, water, ever clear, take this blight and disappear." A spray of thick fluid flowed over Jason, winding up and down his body like liquid mercury. His skin glowed red and the spell went up in steam.

"Oh dear. It appears Nickelova expected my intervention."

"B—but, you can try something else, right?" Laina placed a hand on Gerty's shoulder.

Gerty pursed her lips and tapped her wand on the palm of her hand.

"Let me try," Selene said. Every face turned in her direction.

Laina wrinkled her brow. "This is serious. A dragon fae curse." She glanced at Silas, a shadow of condescension on her features. "Tell her, Silas."

Selene interrupted before Silas could say a word. "The artifacts of the Fireborn Primary were given to us by the goddess herself, along with the knowledge of how to use them. I've been trained for this."

"I thought that was all legend. Have you actually broken a curse before?" Silas asked.

Selene sighed, then reluctantly shook her head. "Well, no. Not in actual practice. But I know how."

Gerty gestured toward Jason. "She can't make this worse. If anything, it will give me a chance to think of what to try next."

"Grateful is researching an antidote in her grimoire," Silas said. "We could wait until she comes back."

"Who knows how long that could take?" Gerty stepped away from the bed, guiding Silas to the back of the room with a gentle hand. "Let the girl give it a shot."

The Fireborn alpha met Selene's gaze. "Do it."

Swallowing hard, Selene approached the bed. Was she really about to do this? Anxiety made her mind go blank. She tried to remember the ritual as she set the chest down on the bed beside Jason and opened it. Taking a deep breath, she closed her eyes to steady her nerves. She'd never done this before—only learned about it in theory. And although she was sure she could execute the ritual correctly, if it didn't work, she'd feel like a fool, like her entire life's work was a game.

"Can I have a candle, please?" she asked Laina. "Preferably white."

The princess left for a moment and returned with a thick white pillar, but nothing to light it with.

"Allow me," Gerty said. With a flick of her silver wand, a flame sputtered to life. Selene nodded her thanks. Then she got down to business.

Kneeling beside the bed, she laid both hands on Jason's heart and began to chant in the original language of her people. The series of growls, grunts, and clicks combined with more human syllables was not used anymore, aside from her religious order and the orders of the other packs. But her song was an entreaty unto the goddess, begging for divine intervention.

Selene unbuttoned Jason's shirt as she sang, revealing his chest. The remnants of a broad, muscular physique lay wasted before her, wiry and sunken. He was emaciated by werewolf standards. Curling her lip, she thanked the goddess they'd caught this. Jason had been ill a long time.

With careful fingers, she uncorked a bottle of ink prepared with a single flake of the Primary's dried blood and dipped one of the Fireborn claws into it. Still chanting, she started beneath his navel, drawing a pattern of symbols in bright red, careful not to break the skin. The tribal prayer she designed stretched in a straight line, over his stomach, up his neck, to the center of his forehead. When it was complete, she wiped the claw clean on her own robes with a crisscross motion over her heart and returned it to the box.

The air felt thick to her now and the candle's flame flickered more slowly, although she wondered if the perception was due to her deep meditative state and not a verifiable reality. Was everyone seeing things in slow motion? She retrieved the fang from the box, the same one used to carve the tattoo into Kyle's shoulder, and placed it on Jason's forehead where it shone white like a crescent moon.

Her song grew more urgent. The goddess must intervene. She called upon her from the deepest part of herself, from the purest depths of her heart. Carefully, she removed the last artifact—a strip of the Primary's pelt—and draped it across Jason's chest, over his nipples.

Were her eyes deceiving her, or had Jason's skin taken on a purple glow? This was the part of the ritual when she was supposed to draw the curse from his body and bring it into hers. It was why acolytes and priestesses kept themselves pure. A curse would fizzle and die inside her, or so she'd been told. She passed her hands through the heavy air over his body, chanting and sweeping the purple energy toward her chest.

Rapidly, a longing stirred deep within her, an ache blooming low in her abdomen. What was this wanting? She leaned over Jason, her thoughts going places they'd never gone before. She could picture herself on top of him, riding him. She'd never done that, not with anyone. A memory of her hand threading into his filled her mind. Only, the skin of her hand was much too pale. It wasn't hers at all. This was someone else's memory.

And then she saw something else in her mind: a road, a river, and a place between two mountains. *Come to me*, a woman's voice said. Blue eyes flashed from the face of a blond woman whose ghostly body hovered on the other side of the bed.

Selene ignored the apparition and leaned over to complete the ritual. She ended her song of supplication with a kiss to Jason's mouth. On contact, liquid flame coursed through her closed lips, down her throat, and into her lungs. She gasped, straightening and clutching her throat. The curse twisted inside her, a wormlike sensation that worked through her torso. In her pain and panic, she couldn't remember the last part of the spell. Desperately, she gasped for air, unable to free herself of the dark torment.

End how you began came Artemis's voice in her head. *Every prayer is a circle. Always end the way you began.*

Black spots danced in her vision. Frantically, she turned to the candle and blew. Her breath came out black and ignited the flame as if she'd spit gasoline. Fire flared to the ceiling. Hot, cleansing fire. Once the black breath was burned away, the flame extinguished, dowsing itself in a pool of melted wax.

Instantly, she felt lighter, as if she'd removed a heavy weight from her soul. But the lightness turned into a spinning, floating feeling. She heard Gerty gasp. And then Selene's shoulder slapped the wood floor.

* * *

"What the fuck?" Jason sat up within a ring of gaping faces. Something dropped from his forehead and he caught it in his hand. A giant fang. What the hell was all over him? He smeared the red symbols painted on his torso.

Laina and Silas were struggling beside the bed to help someone from the floor. Jason couldn't see who it was behind the full skirt of Laina's dress. His gaze darted to Gerty whose wrinkled expression gave nothing away but was tight with concern.

"I'm all right," Selene's voice came from between them. The elegant blush colored robe drifted into view as Silas and Laina parted. "Water, please." Gerty nodded and ran for the kitchen.

"What's *she* doing here?" Jason asked. "Why is everyone staring? And why the hell am I in Laina's bed?"

Silas growled. "*She* just saved your life." His brother cradled Selene's elbow as she swayed on her feet.

While Jason tried to wrap his head around that tidbit, Laina stood and retrieved a towel from the bathroom, tossing it to him. "You caught something from the dragon fae you had sex with, Jason, and in this case, you'd be better off with syphilis. She cursed you."

Gerty returned with the water and Selene took a long drink before speaking.

"She was trying to lure him somewhere," Selene said. "I saw a road, a river, and two mountains. I saw her beckoning me… I mean, him. When the curse was inside me, I could see what he saw. She was luring him to her."

"Is this true?" Silas asked Jason.

After a long deep inhale, Jason admitted to himself that he could no longer keep his encounter a secret. "Yes. Nickelova came to me the other night, possessed a woman I was with, and told me she needed me. She placed the vision of that place in my head."

The others made a series of shocked gasps and grunts. Jason rolled his eyes toward the ceiling. Crap, he'd hoped to avoid this.

"You knew about this? And you didn't think it was important enough to tell us?" Silas bared his teeth, a dark rumble coming from deep within his chest.

"I had it under control. Besides, I wasn't positive she was real. It might have been a nightmare." The lie rolled off his tongue easily. Her lips around his cock had been real enough.

"So where is this place?" Laina quirked a brow. "Maybe we should pay Nickelova a visit."

"I wouldn't do that," Gerty said. "Attacking a dragon fae in her mountain is like attacking a woodland fae in her tree. You'll never make it out alive."

"Even if we could, I have no idea where her mountain is. I recognize the road as Route 9, and it's

Stone Eagle River, but there are no mountains in that area," Selene said.

"No mountains you can see," said Gerty. "Dragon fae can't make a mountain but they can use magic to bend space. My guess is that if Jason follows her clues, she's left him a portal that will take him to her mountain, wherever that may be."

"I'll go," Silas said.

Gerty snorted. "Suicide. Do you think she'd let just anyone reach her? And if she did, do you believe for a second it wouldn't be a trap?"

"So, Jason has to go," Laina said. "Or we have to lure her out."

Selene met the princess's gaze and wet her lips before speaking. "But... Jason can't go."

"What? Why?" Laina asked.

Jason squirmed as Selene's gaze shifted to him, cutting right through him.

"He won't be able to say no to her," Selene said. "You'll lose him."

In righteous indignation, Jason bound from the bed, his finger pointing at Selene's chest. "You don't even know me. You have no idea what I can and cannot do. I would never put the pack at risk. I'd die first. Who the hell do you think you are?"

Selene's chin dropped and she took interest in the floor.

Five fingers slapped the center of Jason's chest, Silas's hand bringing him to a full stop. "She's not the problem here."

Jason looked at his brother. "If you want me to go, Silas, I'll go. I'm ready."

Silas's lips pressed into a flat line. "Why do you feel he can't do this, Selene?"

Jason tried to protest but Silas held up a hand.

"When his curse was inside me, I saw what Jason saw and felt what Jason felt when Nickie… Nickelova cursed him. He wanted to… deny her… when she possessed the woman in his apartment. He couldn't. His vice is too strong."

"You don't know what you're talking about." Jason charged her again, stopping a half inch from her face. The movement was threatening enough to cause Selene to shiver.

"Your aura is almost entirely black, Jason." Selene's voice was as wispy as spiderwebs. "If you continue as you have been, you will succumb to the darkness within and there will be no way for any of us to save you."

Jason glared at her. Goddess, her eyes were beautiful, pale violet with flecks of silver when the light hit them just right. He wanted to clock her in the jaw for what she was doing to him. But it was like finding a kitten drinking your milk. Part of you wanted to swat it away and another part wanted to give it a good cuddle. Yet he couldn't allow himself to be sucked in or manipulated by her beauty.

"I can manage my own darkness, thank you very much," he said, the corner of his mouth turning up. "Maybe it's you who needs to make peace with your dark side. You seem a little obsessed with mine."

"Gerty, is there a way to lure a dragon fae from her mountain?" Silas asked, changing tack.

"Hmm. Not exactly." Gerty cocked her head. "A dragon fae's magic comes from her heart. It isn't coincidence that she decided to help Alex. She loved him, which made her vulnerable. Whatever relationship she had with Jason, it was powerful enough for her to come to him when she needed help. She may come for him again."

"And when she does? How do we stop her?" Laina asked.

Gerty's eyes landed on Jason. "When she comes for him, he needs to be ready."

* * * * *

Every part of Selene's body felt heavy as if someone had injected liquid concrete into her bloodstream. She wavered slightly, slight enough that only Jason noticed. He was glaring at her, unblinking. He did not steady her or ask if she was okay.

Silas placed his hands on his hips. "Gerty is right. Jason needs to be ready when Nickelova returns. We can't set a trap for her if he's going to cave to her seduction."

"I'm not going to cave," Jason yelled. "I'm telling you, this… this girl doesn't know what she's talking about." He pointed a hand at Selene.

Laina smoothed the front of her wedding dress. "Your vice is out of control. We've all known it for a while now. Nickelova simply took advantage of it."

"Says the woman who married her vice." Jason's face reddened with anger. "I do not have a problem."

"Then what was the ring for?" Laina countered.

Jason frantically checked his hand. "Where is it?"

"Grateful Knight destroyed it. It was killing you."

"It wasn't killing me—it was helping me. I was quitting my vice. I haven't had sex in days thanks to that ring."

"Days? It's only been a day and a half since you were with Nickelova." Silas ran his hands through his bushy hair.

"It would have worked."

"You passed out, Jason. You were barely breathing. Whatever that ring was doing, it wasn't a long-term solution. Laina knows what she's talking about. Your vice is out of control. You deny it now, but you admitted as much to me yourself at the rehearsal."

"Silas—" Jason started.

"Shut the fuck up." Silas puffed out his chest and went full alpha on Jason, who seemed to deflate slightly.

Selene narrowed her eyes on Jason. There was one last thing she hadn't told Silas, hoping that Jason would rise to the occasion and do it himself. But the defensiveness coming from him made it clear that wasn't going to happen. "Nickelova wants Jason to come to her. The curse I broke was an ultimatum. If he didn't come of his own free will, his vice would make him her slave. Every time he had sex, he'd give up more of his free will. She's going to expect him to come to her… soon."

Jason shook his head, his eyes rolling. "This is none of your business, Selene."

Silas ignored his brother and turned toward Gerty. "Nickelova doesn't know we've broken her curse. But she will. The longer Jason stays away, the more she'll suspect something's gone wrong."

Gerty glared at Jason over her bifocals. "If she hears he's gone back to his old ways but hasn't come to her, she'll know her curse has been undone. I highly recommend against that. The best course of action is to make Nickelova believe that he is still under her curse for as long as possible."

"Which was why I was using the ring. It was helping me stay sober," Jason said.

"It was also killing you." Selene fisted her hands. "I can help you break your vice without dark magic.

With the help of the goddess, I can lead you through a program to end your addiction and make you strong enough to face Nickelova when she comes for you."

Jason growled. "I don't need your help. Frankly, you've done enough."

"What exactly does this program entail?" Silas asked.

"Daily meditation, prayer, diet, and the practice of ritual aura cleansing—"

"No way." Jason scanned her from head to toe.

Laina huffed. "This is your life we're talking about! Selene is offering you a way out. It's not forever, Jason. Just until we can capture or kill Nickelova and Alex."

"Laina's right," Silas said. "Every day you are out there living your old life is a danger to the pack. She'll come for you again. You need to be prepared when she does."

"What? What are you saying?" Jason rubbed his head.

"It's the only way," Laina said.

Silas set his jaw. "Selene, it would honor the pack if you would help my brother break his vice."

"Hello? I am still standing here," Jason said. "And I said *no way*."

Silas shook his head slowly. "And I'm alpha and this is my call. I'm putting you in Selene's care, full-time, until we get this thing figured out."

"What?" Jason and Selene said together.

Selene cleared her throat. "The program does not require my full-time care. I believe it can be accomplished with a half-day session three times a week."

Silas shook his head again. "If I could count on my brother to follow your program, that would be good enough. Unfortunately, I don't trust him—"

"Silas!" Jason pleaded.

"I'm sorry, brother, but you know as well as I do that you'll be out the door and in the arms of the first woman you see."

"What are you saying? You're assigning Selene as my babysitter?" Jason gaped at his brother in horror.

"More like your warden. I want Selene to stay with you, full-time."

"But I live in Sanctuary at Rivergate Manor. The *Preotka*—" Selene's heart raced. Surely Silas wasn't suggesting she *live* with Jason. After all, the man looked as if he wanted to kill her at the moment.

"*Preotka* Artemis will be receptive to your assignment when she understands the safety of the pack is at risk. I assume Jason can't stay with you in Sanctuary."

"No." She chuckled softly. "Males are not allowed."

"Then you will stay with Jason until he's better. Do we all understand each other?" Silas looked between Selene and Jason.

Selene nodded.

"You can't do this to me. I have work. I have a life." Jason bared his teeth and planted his hands on his hips.

"The faster you get with the program, the faster you can have both of those things back," Silas said.

"You fucking bastard." Jason swung a fist at Silas's head, barely missing Selene in the process. Silas caught his fist, palm slapping knuckles loud enough to make Selene tense away from the crackle of testosterone in the room.

"Back down, brother, or things are going to get worse for you. Much, much worse."

He lowered his fist.

"I'm going to call Artemis and make sure we're on the same page about Selene. I'll meet you out front and escort you back to your condo. Selene, take your time getting your things together. I'll wait with Jason until you can join us." He nodded his good-bye.

"I need to find Kyle," Laina said, hoisting up the skirt of her wedding dress and following after Silas. Gerty gave one last sideways glance toward Jason before making her own exit.

Although he didn't say a word, Jason's jaw tightened as he looked at Selene, his gaze raking over her forehead, nose, and lips with barely contained repulsion.

She reached a trembling hand out to Jason's clenched fist. He jerked away from her, but she gently gripped his wrist and wrenched open his fingers. He was still clenching the Primary's fang. She slid the artifact from his palm and carefully returned it to the box. She gathered the pelt that Jason had cast aside when he awoke, folded it carefully, and returned it to its place among the other artifacts, checking and double-checking that everything was where it belonged before closing and locking the sacred chest.

"You don't have to do this," Jason said. "You could refuse. My brother wouldn't deny you, especially if you asked Artemis to back you up."

"Why would I do that?" Selene said, meeting his gaze. "You need me. I can help you."

Jason stepped in close, his body blocking the window and casting a dark shadow over her. "You don't want to live with me, Selene." His finger landed on her chest and traced the smear of blood that remained there from the ritual. "It's not safe. I'm a bad man with a vice. You're a woman. You wouldn't want to put yourself at risk, would you?"

Narrowing her eyes, Selene squared her shoulders, lifting the box from the bed in such a way that it banged into Jason's stomach. He took a step back with a resounding *oomph*.

"I don't believe for a second that you are capable of hurting me. And if you even think about taking your vice out on me, think again. I may be a woman, but I'm not as defenseless as I seem."

"Every woman has her vulnerabilities." His threatening tone made her spine tingle.

Exhausted from the ritual and in no mood to argue, she leaned forward and whispered into his ear, "Just remember, I saw into your soul. I know what you did with Nickelova… and other things. I know who you really are, Jason Flynn. Before you even think about messing with me, you'd better consider your own vulnerabilities."

EIGHT

On the way back to his condominium, Jason had half a mind to drive directly to the security office of the Bachman Building and tell them that Silas, who trailed a car length behind him, was a stalker. He'd enjoy watching some half-trained, underpaid, overcaffeinated human in a blue uniform interrogate his big brother. Unfortunately, all it would take was a direct alpha command from Silas and life could get even worse… fast.

One word, said with the right inflection and eye contact, and Jason would be forced to obey or face the consequences—namely a body that burned as if he had acid in his veins. There'd been rumors of alphas throughout history punishing their wolves by making them kneel on concrete until they bled or forcing them to take a hammer to their own hand. Silas had never done anything like that, but he was capable of it. Most people didn't realize it, but the guy had anger issues. Darkness lay beneath the buddy-cop exterior.

Silas would do anything to protect his pack, and that included torturing his little brother. Jason had no choice but to go along with this ridiculous plan. Or else.

It wasn't the program itself he was dreading. It was Selene. Giving up sex would be difficult, both physically and mentally, he was sure. He'd lied before to Laina about going two weeks without it. It had been years since he'd gone more than two days. But Selene… Selene, with her perfect skin and her holier-than-thou attitude… Her fucking virtue was a constant reminder of everything he wasn't. And now she was in charge. *Sesame Street* twenty-four hours a day.

He appreciated her saving his life. He did. And part of him regretted not thanking her for that particular service. But how creepy was it that she'd seen and felt the depravity going on inside his brain. She'd likely never allow him to forget the filth he was. How he was dark to her light, tainted to her clean, unworthy to her admirable. And she'd be right there to watch him squirm as his vice tortured him from the inside out.

"Get out." Silas knocked on his driver's side window, looking peeved.

Jason turned off the ignition and crawled from the car. "How about a nice hospital stay? There's a rehab institute in Arizona where a popular pro golfer found some success."

"No. You need Selene. She understands the difference between a human addiction and a werewolf vice."

"And so do you, Silas. You know I won't be able to give it up permanently. My wolf will go mad."

Silas said nothing. They stepped into the elevator and Silas pressed the button for the top floor: Jason's penthouse.

"It's not like I actually have a problem. I understand you need me to prove I can go without sex. You want to be sure I can say no to Nickelova, but this isn't like snorting cocaine or shooting up heroin. I can't give up sex any more than I could give up eating or drinking. Not long term. My wolf needs it to survive."

Wordlessly, Silas stepped off the elevator, waiting patiently for Jason to unlock his door.

"It was the curse that caused all the trouble. Not my vice," Jason said. "I don't have a problem, just a manageable condition. I can stop on my own anytime I want. I don't need Selene."

Silas closed the door behind them.

"Have you listened to a word I've said?" Jason stared at his brother in frustration.

"You have a different woman every night of the week but couldn't get a date for your sister's wedding," Silas said matter-of-factly.

"It wasn't a convenient time—"

"We schedule our family events around your *sessions* because you are intolerable to be around otherwise."

"Understandable, I'd say, given that I have a metaphysical need for sex."

Silas rubbed the base of his neck. "You couldn't turn down the woman who almost killed us… almost killed me… just a few months ago."

"She caught me off guard. Look, I know I need more control but I can do it myself. I don't need help."

Silas ran his tongue along his upper teeth. "Want a drink before Selene gets here?"

Blowing out a deep breath, Jason nodded. "I'd love one." The crawling feeling was back, under his skin, and his suit felt heavy and constricting. He removed his jacket and unbuttoned his top two buttons.

Although Jason kept a large variety of liquors stocked in the bar next to the fireplace, Silas went straight for the bourbon, pouring two glasses of Pappy Van Winkle. Jason didn't waste a second. He tossed the stuff back like it was lemonade and held his glass out for another. Silas obliged.

"Selene will be here soon. There's something I want to talk to you about."

"What?"

Silas made eye contact and held it. "You will not leave this apartment without Selene's permission."

It was an alpha command. The words sifted through Jason's cells and formed a heavy weight over his heart as his body processed the command. He snorted derisively. "You bastard."

"I didn't like the way you looked at her in the cabin. Almost like you hated her. You need her, Jason. Don't fuck this up by pushing her away."

"Thanks for the vote of confidence." Jason slammed the glass down on the counter. "I'm tired. Being brought back from the dead can do that to a person. I'm going to bed."

"Jason—"

He turned on his heel and headed for his room, leaving Silas standing by the bar.

* * * * *

Goddess, he was an asshole. Locked in his room, Jason stared at the ceiling, the cruel ache of unfulfilled need gathering like a two-ton weight between his thighs. He'd heard Selene arrive and Silas leave, but instead of welcoming her or thanking her for saving his life, he'd stayed locked in his room, brooding over his predicament.

Why he'd thought he could sleep, he wasn't sure. His cock had an entirely different plan and the long, thick length of him was currently pitching a tent in his covers. He stroked a hand over his sunken abs and palmed that sucker, stroking himself slowly from base to tip. It was a small reprieve, like a sip of air to a drowning man, but he'd suffered under his vice long enough to know the relief would be short-lived. Self-gratification tended to sate his inner beast for a short time, only to be followed by an increased desire for sex. It was like putting out the fire with gasoline.

As he arched his back and rolled his hips, pumping harder and faster, the build of pleasure felt like a roller coaster chugging toward that first major drop. He went over the edge, free-falling down the other side with a clear view of the broken track ahead.

And then *she* was there. It wasn't his hand but Nickelova's moving against him. He rolled onto his side and bound from the bed, just barely making it to the bathroom before self-loathing turned his stomach. He heaved but there was nothing inside him to purge. When he was done, he checked his room, under the bed, in his closet. Thankfully, Nickie had been a figment of his imagination this time. Even the thought of her made everything feel dirty, tainted.

He turned on the shower and let the heat build. Stripping out of his pajamas, he stepped into the scalding water and scrubbed. His wolf was already revved up again, and as predicted, the edge of his need was sharper than before. He scrubbed harder, trading the need for pleasure for the sting of pain. Nickelova was on the edge of every orgasm, it seemed, curse or not. As he tipped his head back into the spray, he swore. He would not let her win. No fucking way.

* * * * *

Hours later, Jason lay on his floor, alternating sit-ups and push-ups in an effort to distract himself from his vice. Only problem was, he could smell Selene. Ripe mango and vanilla. She was right outside his door. There were other smells: food, breakfast he assumed. But his brain dismissed everything except the scent of the female. His inner wolf paced restlessly, eager to be in the presence of a woman. "Not this one," Jason said under his breath. "This one is seriously off-limits."

Unlocking the door, he passed through the short corridor into the great room, frowning when he saw a pallet of blankets on the floor next to the sofa beside the ugliest brown plaid bag he'd ever seen. Was that her luggage? Had she slept on the floor last night? He clenched a fist against his stomach. Why hadn't Silas set her up in the guestroom?

After a cursory check of the room, he saw the shape of her seated silhouette through the morning dew on the glass door to his balcony. Quietly, he slipped outside. She'd exchanged her silk robe for jeans that bagged in all the wrong places and a T-shirt he found wholly unacceptable. Her complicated chignon was gone, replaced with a ponytail.

Legs crisscrossed on the concrete, her eyes were closed, her back straight, hands folded in her lap. He stepped around her. That couldn't be comfortable. It was cold out here, the spring chill hanging in the morning air. She should have a mat or better yet, a chair under her.

"Why didn't you sleep in the guest room last night?" he said sharply. More sharply than he'd intended.

Her eyes opened, the sunrise constricting her pupils and turning her irises an intense shade of violet. He had to consciously stop himself from gasping. His lips parted and for a moment he just took her in. A flock of black birds chose that moment to take off from the roof, their flapping wings and morning caws contrasting the weighty silence of her presence. It was as if she owned the air around her. The effect was intense.

"Good morning," she said, a soft, pleasant smile warming her face. "I wasn't comfortable settling into your guestroom without your permission. I'm here to help you, not to make myself at home."

Jason tried to respond but the words stuck in his throat. He wiped a hand over his mouth and cleared the thickness from his vocal cords. "I… I can't have you sleeping on the floor. Come on." Roughly, he reached out and grabbed her by the arm, pulling her off the concrete and through the glass door. Aside from a guttural grunt, she didn't protest, though he suspected he was hurting her.

Moving like this, dragging her behind him like a child, kept him from thinking of her as a woman. He couldn't afford to look at her too closely or to consider the way her cotton T-shirt hugged her curves, not with his wolf pressing against his skin. Not with the crawling need that had kept him up all night.

He swept her ugly brown bag into the crook of his arm and lifted the pallet from the floor. He didn't stop until they were standing in his guest room, the plush gray of the comforter absorbing the impact of her things. "Until I can convince Silas to send you away, you'll stay in here. Understand?"

"Okay," she said softly.

"It would help if you told Silas I don't need you."

"But you do need me."

He eyed her from head to toe. "No, sweetheart. Look at you. This whole thing… it's way out of your league."

"Look at me?" Her brow puckered. "What's that supposed to mean?"

"You're not exactly dressed to sit at the adult table." He shoved his hands into his pockets and rocked back on his heels. "Come on. You're celibate. You know as well as I do you've bitten off more than you can chew. Do yourself a favor and ask to be removed from my case." He backed out the door.

"I'll do no such thing!" Selene protested, but Jason wasn't listening.

He'd stopped short when he saw the source of the breakfast smells. The kitchen counter was laden with pancakes, scrambled eggs, bacon, fresh coffee.

"I made you breakfast," Selene said from behind him. "It should still be hot."

He sighed. Most of the time the hollow feeling inside his abdomen was suppressed, hidden under the layers of constant wanting that drove his every decision. But now, seeing it all there, he almost felt hungry. "I don't usually eat breakfast."

"No kidding. Your refrigerator was a graveyard of half-empty take-out containers."

"Where did you even find the food?"

"I brought it. It's part of the regimen. You'll eat six times a day. Your body needs to be strong and healthy if we're going to beat this thing."

"Healthy." Jason's eyes drifted to the bar near the fireplace and widened when he found it empty. "What happened to the wine? The Macallan? The Pappy Bourbon?"

"I had to get rid of it." Selene shrugged.

Jason's hands dug into his hair. "Thousands of dollars…"

Her laugh rang through the room like a bell. He looked at her in horror. Was she really laughing at his pain?

"Relax," she finally said. "Silas took it for safekeeping. You can have it back when you're better."

He dropped into a chair at the white oak table and rubbed his forehead. "So… the acolyte has a sense of humor. A cruel but existent sense of humor."

She crossed her right foot behind her left and bowed, her ponytail flopping over her shoulder. The movement made her look young and light like she was made of air rather than skin and bone. "We have a joke among acolytes."

He slouched. "Let's hear it."

"A werewolf, a vampire, and an acolyte walk into a bar. The bartender asks, 'What'll it be?' The werewolf orders a beer. The vampire orders a pint of blood. What does the acolyte order?"

"I don't know, what?"

"A candle to light for the souls of the vampire and the werewolf."

"That's the worst joke I've ever heard."

"Well, if we were comedians we would have chosen a different vocation." She strode into the kitchen and started loading a plate.

"What is that in the eggs?"

"Onions, peppers, tomato, spinach. It helps with hormonal balance."

As she swayed in front of the counter, she added pancakes to the heaping pile forming on the plate in her hands. He shifted in his chair, his cock kicking. His inner wolf stretched and lowered his head, stalking her every movement. Breathing deeply, he sorted out her mango and vanilla scent.

Selene didn't seem to notice his lascivious stare. She plopped the full plate in front of him and handed him a fork. "Please don't take this the wrong way but I've noticed you've lost weight," she said. "Do you eat regularly?" Her voice was full of caring and concern, but all Jason's cock heard was a sultry murmur.

"Hmm?" He stared at the round curve of her hip.

She wandered back toward the food and started loading another plate. "Eating? Have you been… regularly?"

"Uh. I've been busy. Work and things. Plus, I don't cook." His lids drooped as he followed the line of her body from thigh, to shoulder, to that long caramel-colored ponytail that swung behind her. He'd like to roll his hand in the length of it, tug her head back, and explore her mouth with his.

She cleared her throat. "Is something wrong?"

"Not at all."

"You are… um… staring at me." She plated the food and walked to the table, taking the seat across from him.

"How could I not stare?" Jason flashed his practiced smile. "You're exquisite."

For a moment, she blinked at him, her body leaning closer as she studied his face and inhaled deeply through her nose. Then all at once she broke from his gaze and shook herself. "I'm also celibate, Jason. Your condition is going to make you see things that aren't there for a while. You might even see me as a potential target of your vice. But that's not who I am."

He swallowed a bite of breakfast, fixating on her full lips.

"Who are you then?" he asked.

"I'm the one who decides when you get to leave this apartment." There wasn't a hint of humor in her voice, her back straight, her jaw tight.

Under her unwavering gaze, Jason continued to eat, surprised how hungry he actually was. "What's in this? There's an aftertaste."

"It's an herb designed to support the healing process. The bitterness you taste is valerian root. It has a calming effect on your sympathetic nervous system."

"You're trying to drug me?"

"I'm trying to make it so you can sleep." She lowered her voice and turned her attention toward her food. "I heard you last night."

He swallowed the food in his mouth, mortified at the possibility she'd heard him pleasure himself. "What exactly did you hear?"

"You were showering in the middle of the night," she said matter-of-factly. "I presume the physical withdrawal symptoms were to blame. Racing pulse, sweating, crawling skin."

"I thought you said you'd never done this before?" In fact, he'd had all of those symptoms at one point or another last night.

"Not with a vice like yours. I have never treated a sexual vice, but I have studied alcohol addiction in werewolves. There are similarities."

God she was beautiful, but she addressed him like a toddler. Was she judging him? Pitying him? The way she'd brushed off his advances was cold as ice, rigid, all kinds of palm up and no way. It made him horny as hell. Not only was she beautiful, she'd proved herself feisty. How he longed to tame her, bring her to her knees.

He took another bite, enjoying the fantasy that played out in his head. Selene on her knees. But even as he reveled in it, the vision warped from a sexual one to something else entirely. Selene on her knees in her ceremonial robes, praying to the goddess. *Fuck him.* She was an acolyte. What was he thinking, lusting after her? The guilt drove into him like a freight train.

"Once you're finished, we'll begin stage one," she said.

"What's stage one?"

Selene's violet stare cut straight to his soul. "I take you apart, so I can put you back together."

NINE

Selene hadn't meant her words to sound threatening, but from the way Jason's face paled and his fork hit his plate, they fell sharp and heavy on her target. What was she doing, saying it like that? Only, he'd shaken her to the core. That chiseled face, the charming smile, the way his gaze raked over her… His words and actions promised delights she'd only dreamed about. She'd caught herself leaning into him, practically begging for his lips. She'd smelled his desire for her, musk and spice, a heavenly scent that made her insides want to liquefy. Thank the goddess she'd caught herself before things went too far.

"Take me apart?" Jason said. "What will that entail?"

The scent of desire was gone, replaced by the sharp tang of fear. Good. She pushed her fruit around her plate. "Attachments like yours don't develop overnight. This started with your wolf, true, but most vices are harmless, mild. Yours has morphed into a twenty-four-hours-a-day, seven-days-a-week human addiction. For that to happen, there must have been a trigger. My job is to find that trigger, that cancer hiding in the dark recesses of your subconscious, and bring it into the light where we can address it directly."

With a shake of his head, Jason laughed. "No. Selene, it's just a vice. It's a vice I've indulged, sure. Why wouldn't I? Because of Nickelova, I need to quit for a while, but I'm not addicted, not in the human sense."

"No? So, your need for sex exists only *before* the full moon, when your wolf is most active? Strange you weren't able to turn down Nickelova so soon *after* the last shift when your wolf should have been buried deep within your subconscious."

He shifted, leaned back in his chair like a reticent toddler, and crossed his arms over his chest.

"You don't have to answer me. I know the truth. Silas filled me in on your… schedule and how it has increased over the years." She sipped her coffee and waited for him to deny it. He didn't. "So what we need to do is unravel exactly why this vice was able to get its hooks into you so deeply. The root of every vice is an unfulfilled emotional need."

"You're going to psychoanalyze me? What, do I lie on the couch and tell you how I lost my virginity?"

"I'm not a psychiatrist. I'm an acolyte for the priesthood. I don't want to tap into your mind. I want to tap into your soul."

If he'd been pale before, his current chalky corpse color redefined the term. He cleared his throat. "No."

She sat back, rubbing her palms on her thighs. "You can't put me off forever. I'll call Silas if I have to."

Jason's eyes tightened at the corners, seeming to size up the threat. "I'll need to do some work before we start. I have a few pressing e-mails I have to review."

"Can't it wait?"

"No. I'm an angel investor. People are counting on me."

She looked at him blankly.

"Our parents left us a large fortune when they died. My job is to use my portion of that inheritance to invest in businesses that need capital… after I vet them first."

"You just give them the money?"

"In exchange for a percentage of future profits. So, you see, as much as I'd like to dive right into your therapy, I have an obligation to my clients that comes first."

"How long will it take you?"

He stood and placed his plate in the sink. "A few hours. I'm sure you can, um, touch my soul later, right? Or tomorrow?"

She shook her head. "Jason—"

"Then it's settled."

Selene sighed heavily as he retreated into his bedroom, the click of the door locking behind him signaling the end of their conversation.

* * * * *

"Tap into my goddamned soul? Over my dead body." If there was one good thing about Selene sharing her intended goals for the day, it was a temporary damper on his libido. He couldn't think of anything he desired less than to have Little Miss Virtuous poking around in his emotional attic. Jason plopped down at his desk and flipped open his laptop. He wasn't hiding anything per se, but it was the principle of the thing. Anyone with any sense of privacy would balk at the notion.

He opened his e-mail and concentrated on reviewing the latest batch of financials from his scout, Andrew. He had a good feeling about this new company, Spackles.

Set up a meeting with Spackles' executive team, he texted Andrew.

The return text came back almost immediately. *Perfect. I had a feeling you'd see the potential. How about Friday?*

Jason looked over his shoulder at the door.

Actually, I'm having a medical procedure. Next week?

Is everything okay? Anything I should know about?

Routine.

Thank god. We need you healthy. Baby needs a new pair of shoes.

Jason laughed. Of course Andrew wanted to rush this one. His commission would set him up for the year.

Next week.

I'm on it, boss. Take care.

Tossing his phone on the desk, he moved on to the next e-mail, another company, another scout, another set of financials. What Selene didn't realize was, when it came to his business, there was always work to do. He could do this all day, all night if he had to. He supposed if he worked long enough, he'd prove to her he could break this vice on his own without the need for any religious mumbo jumbo.

Only, as the day wore on, Jason's vice had other things in mind. Although he stared at his computer screen, his wolf sent him a crystal-clear fantasy of hooking his fingers into the waistband of Selene's jeans, sliding them over her hips, and burying his face between her thighs. Mangos and vanilla, that's what she smelled like. He wondered if the scent would be stronger or more defined between her legs. Would her skin taste sweet? Was her flesh as soft as it looked?

He got to his feet and paced the room. She said she was celibate, but she wouldn't be here if she wasn't curious. He could teach her to like it. *Fuck.* How could he be expected to maintain his distance with a woman who was in his apartment so willingly? He felt like a spider with a fly caught in his web, a fly he wasn't supposed to touch. Yeah, right.

He paced faster, a growl stirring in his chest. Silas should've known better than to send a woman. Of course, all werewolf priestesses *were* women, but that was just more of a reason why he should have been allowed to face his demons on his own.

Demons.

Jason dug through the drawer of his nightstand. His hand fell on a small box, a box with a snake on the lid. He hipped the drawer closed and crossed to his desk. As far as he knew, Grateful had destroyed the ring, but that didn't mean Ryker wouldn't have a replacement. Turning the box over in his hand, he referred to the sticker with the Lost Things logo and phone number stuck to the bottom and started to dial the number… and stopped.

He could smell her. She'd walked past his room. His erection kicked and his body ached with need. A whimper broke his lips.

Pocketing his phone, he glared at the door. It was too late for rings or potions. He needed sex, and he needed it now.

TEN

Selene squared her shoulders and screwed up her courage. Even though Jason was a royal, she couldn't allow him to push her aside. She was here for a reason, and she was going to follow through with her commitment to Silas and to Artemis. The problem was, every time she looked at Jason—those piercing green eyes and that perfectly designed face—she felt a wave of inappropriate attraction. She was fairly sure it was an echo, left over from the ritual she'd performed. When she'd taken Nickelova's curse into her body, she'd had a taste of what it would be like to be with Jason, and she'd be lying to herself if she said it wasn't the single most pleasurable feeling she'd ever encountered in her work.

But she couldn't think about that. He'd never get better locked in his room. In fact, he'd missed lunch and dinner. His growing physical hunger might exacerbate his symptoms. And there was more at stake here than just helping him gain control of his vice. Her future as pack priestess was on the line. It was time for the two of them to start down his road to recovery.

"Jason?" She rapped on his door. "You need to come out now. Have something to eat. Begin your therapy."

Nothing.

"I'm becoming concerned. It's been over twelve hours since your last meal. I need to know you're okay in there." She knocked again.

Nothing.

"Jason, you're scaring me. I'm coming in." She tried the doorknob. Locked. Of course it was. The lever-style door handle was the type mainly designed for decoration. Not exactly tamper proof. She removed a bobby pin from her hair and stuck it in the tiny hole next to the lever. She heard a pop and the handle gave way. But she'd barely had enough time to pull her hand away when the door flew open. She staggered back, dodging the swinging wood by mere inches.

From the belly of the dark room, Jason stalked toward her like a predator, chin tucked, shoulders hunched, tracking her every move. She barely recognized him. His presence had devolved to something purely animal.

"Jason, your eyes. Your wolf is too close to the surface."

He inhaled deeply in response.

She hurried backward, hands raised. A growl rumbled from deep within his chest as he pursued her, his longer legs closing the space between them in no time. She scampered for the door like a rabbit fleeing from a hunter, a creeping apprehension spreading through her body. Jason's skin gave off a sweaty sheen and his pupils were dilated. Selene wondered if he was fully sentient. And the smell, oh goddess, the scent of his arousal was a complex spice in the air that made her heart race and not just from fear.

Her backside bumped into the wall next to the door. "Jason, stop!"

He pounced. His larger body slammed hers into the wall, his long tapered fingers wrapping around her throat until his thumb stroked her pulse. "Let me out," he rasped into her ear. His voice was not his own, more feral than human. The sound made her scalp tingle.

She couldn't speak but she shook her head. No. She couldn't let him leave.

His knee pitched forward, wedging itself between her legs and thumping the wall behind her. In this position, his thigh grazed her crotch, his body heat covering her like the world's sexiest blanket. His weight pressed against her chest as he brought his lips to her ear again. "Let me out, now."

She attempted to push him away but even with his diminished body weight, he was stronger than her.

Her hands shoved ineffectively at his shoulders, the feel of his lean muscle against her palms awakening that thing within her she'd fought so hard to suppress. Why did he have to look the way he did? Against her wishes, her body responded, a rush of heat flooding her core.

He inhaled deeply. Shit, he could smell her excitement. He let go of her throat and caught her wrists in one hand, pressing them against the wall above her head. Was it possible for him to get any closer without being inside of her? The thought made her insides quiver. His breath coiled against her lips.

All at once, everything changed. She was no longer an acolyte of twenty-five in Jason's apartment. She was fifteen, on a dirty mattress in the back of a truck stop, and a foul man was holding her wrists. The memory slammed into her, shaking her to her core. Any desire she'd felt quickly turned to fear, and her breath came in ragged pants.

"Go!" she shouted. "I give you permission to leave."

Jason retracted immediately, grabbed his keys from the small table in the foyer, and left without another word. Selene pitched forward, catching her hands on her denim-clad knees. The walls wavered, the air hot and oppressive. No. It wasn't the walls or the apartment. It was her. She was under attack from the inside. Panic. Anxiety.

She closed her eyes and thought of her anchor, that one supremely happy memory with the power to bring her back from the brink of a full-blown meltdown. It had been a long time since she'd needed to use it. But with her ghosts circling, the trauma of her past creeping into the present, she needed to employ the coping skills she thought she'd perfected long ago.

When she called on the memory, it was always the color blue she remembered first: a shade deeper than royal blue, but not quite navy. Edged in white, it was the color of a wall… no, a room. The blue room. Rivergate Manor. She was too dirty to be in that room but the man who had brought her there had told her to wait. He'd seemed nice.

"Hello, dear." Artemis's gray spirals seemed to pick up a hint of the blue, further emphasizing the color of her eyes. Selene thought she looked like an angel. "My friend tells me he found you living under a bridge. Where is your family?"

Selene shook her head.

"My friend tells me he saw you shift last night."

Hugging herself, Selene's eyes widened.

"You didn't think I'd know about the shift? Oh, yes. I'm a werewolf too. We all are wolves here." Artemis sat down on an upholstered bench near the fireplace. "Are your parents wolves?" she asked softly.

Selene shook her head.

"Did they kick you out of the house?"

How did she know? Selene looked down at her feet.

"It happens more than you might think. Lycanthropy is genetic. On occasion, werewolves breed with humans and the gene is suppressed. It might rear its head two or three generations from the source. This can be terrifying to people unfamiliar with our kind."

"They're gone now. They moved," Selene said, remembering the day she'd come home from high school to find an empty house and no forwarding address. "I haven't seen them in almost a year."

"That's a long time to be living on the street. What are you… fifteen?"

"Sixteen. I'll be seventeen in January."

Artemis nodded. "How would you like this to be your new home? You can stay here with us and I'll take care of you. We'll become your pack."

Selene's eyes darted around the opulent room, from the gilded chandelier to the fireplace with its stone mantle. "Why… would you do that?"

Artemis smiled. "It's what the goddess wants. She sent you to us, and it is our duty to accept her gift."

"The goddess?" Selene laughed, shaking her head.

Artemis took her hand. "Come, my child. Let's find you a room. There will be plenty of time to discuss all of this when you're rested."

Selene emerged from the memory with a deep inhale, opening her eyes. She was a werewolf, an acolyte, a gift from the goddess. She was no victim.

"Oh no, Jason." If anything happened to him, Artemis would be so disappointed in her. He was her responsibility and obviously not in his right mind. She sprinted into his room, looking for anything that might give her a clue to where he might go.

Next to his laptop, a box carved out of ebony sat on top of a pile of paperwork. She'd seen the snake on the lid before. Yes, the ring Jason had worn. She flipped it open. Empty, of course. Still, Jason had been toying with the box. Why?

"Lost Things," she read off the label on the bottom. It was worth a try.

She reached for her phone. She was going to need transportation.

* * * * *

"Are you sure you want to be dropped off here, miss?" the Uber driver asked. "This is a bad neighborhood. Real bad. I won't be able to wait for you while you're inside."

Selene heard a high-pitched scream from somewhere down the alley followed by running footsteps that faded with distance. She hesitated. Stacks of books with worn titles waited just inside the front window, only one that she could read from her seat—*The Glory of the Dead.* An antique doll's head with a half-burned face leaned against the stack next to what looked like a human skull.

"I hate the sign," the driver said. "Look at the eyes. Is the little boy lost physically or lost in another way?" The big man shivered.

"I… I don't know," Selene said, glancing at the Lost Things logo.

"Well, it gives me the creeps. Either go in now or I'm charging you for the ride back. I'm not staying here another minute."

She apologized and tipped him a few dollars. Steeling her resolve, she hopped out of the midsize sedan and hurried into the shop. The bell above the door chimed, heralding her entrance.

A man she was sure was a vampire turned from a shelf that held nothing but baskets of bones, sorted by size. He flashed her a little fang before resuming his shopping. The place stank of moldy parchment and bad taxidermy, but Selene shuffled deeper into the store.

"You're in the wrong place, angel," a man's voice said. He seemed to appear out of thin air beside her, dark and menacing. Not dark skinned, just dark. Black hair, black eyes, a complexion with olive undertones, and upturned eyes she couldn't associate with any specific supernatural species or the human race. But his presence was dark as if the night air had become corporal beside her.

"I'm no angel."

"But your soul doesn't belong in this zip code." His voice was burning cinder blocks.

"I… are you the owner of this store?" She held up the box.

"Now… where did you get *that*, angel?"

"From Jason Fl—"

"Shhh. We have a strict privacy policy here. I know of whom you speak. What business is he of yours?"

"I'm supposed to be watching him… helping him. But he went crazy and left his apartment. I need to find him." She lowered her voice. "He's not in his right mind. He might not be safe. Do you know where he is?"

The door chimed—the vampire leaving.

"I know where I told him to go, but it is no place for you, angel. Jason's vice needs to be fed, and with that dragon fae at large, there is only one safe place to do it."

"Where? Can I walk there from here?"

"Not if you want to arrive with a beating heart."

Known for her even temperament, Selene wasn't usually the type of person to act out. But she was tired and scared and woefully sick of the dark man's cryptic language. In one slick motion, she plucked a dagger off a nearby shelf and brought it to his throat, violently gripping the man's upper arm.

"Enough," she said with a growl. "Take me to Jason. Now! He's my responsibility. Whatever this place is, I can handle it."

The man dissolved from her grip. One minute there, the next a pillar of black smoke that smelled of sulfur. He returned to human form a few feet away from her. She lowered the blade.

He rubbed his shoulder where she'd gripped him. "No angel, indeed," he murmured. "Very well, I will take you, but I won't be responsible for the consequences."

ELEVEN

Jason climbed the steps of Maison des Étoilles mechanically, awake but with arms and legs moving toward the bordello without any conscious effort. When he reached the door, it opened of its own volition. A slight figure with silky black hair and long pale limbs welcomed him inside. She was naked other than a grouping of starlike light that hovered over her nipples and dripped like icicles down her abdomen and between her legs. Fae magic.

"Welcome." The smile the fae gave him sparkled unnaturally in the dim light.

"One," he said. He handed her a wad of cash.

She whispered something into a small microphone in a language Jason didn't understand. "Is there a name you'd prefer to be called?

"No names."

She bowed slightly. "As you wish. Follow me." She led him deeper within the dark paneled walls and red velvet of the bordello. "We don't ask your desires here at Maison des Étoilles. Every girl is capable of reading your thoughts. She will adapt the session based on your deepest fantasies."

"How adaptable are they?"

"Within these walls, we can take on the form of anyone, man, woman, or beast. If you'd like multiples, one can become two, but any more require additional help. She'll ring me if she can't accommodate you." The hostess gave him a wink.

"One… woman is all I need. Thank you."

Opening a door for him, she fluttered her lashes in his direction. "As you wish. But please understand, our only goal is to please you. There's no need to hide anything from us here. We are rarely surprised by our guests' deepest desires." She turned and swayed down the hall toward the hostess stand.

He stepped into the room, the light from the hall extinguishing as the door closed behind him. For a moment, he was lost in darkness; then a red light clicked on, illuminating a four-poster bed with a gauzy white canopy. A curvy brunette slunk from the shadows, completely naked except for a black mask that covered most of her face.

"Look at those amber eyes. Someone is hungry," she said. "*Very* hungry. We won't waste another minute." She reached for his belt buckle, her full breasts bobbing with the effort of unbuckling it.

She was good, he had to admit. This was what he desired. A fast, surgical coupling that would appease the wolf and give him control over his life again. It didn't matter what she looked like or what she said or did. That wasn't why he was here.

Naked in a matter of minutes, Jason let his wolf take control. He spun her around and bent her over. The wolf didn't bother with foreplay or asking her name or analyzing his desires. It was instinct. Dominance. Action. He was about to thrust into her when she turned her head, looking at him over her shoulder. Her mask disappeared and the curvy brunette transformed into a long-waisted beauty with caramel tresses and violet eyes that flashed in his direction.

"Selene," he murmured. The change in her appearance did nothing to quell his desire. On the contrary, it ignited a yearning deep within him. No longer did he want a quick fuck. He wanted to touch her. Wanted to feel her silky skin. He reached out, his fingers coasting along soft pale flesh.

Her full lips parted in response, a moan spilling over that perfect pink tongue. She pressed her hips back, but he didn't enter her. Couldn't, although he wanted to. Not Selene. Far from being a pleasurable experience, touching the Selene look-alike triggered shockwaves that rolled through him like a ball of barbed wire. He could take her and it would satisfy his wolf's hunger, but it would also shred him. She was too good. Too pure. And he wasn't worthy. The heavy, sinking feeling in his chest had a name. It was shame, pure and simple.

The Selene look-alike reached for him. "My, my, Selene is a lucky girl."

"Don't do that. Don't say her name."

The woman stopped. "As you wish. Would you like me to be more aggressive? Your thoughts are conflicted."

Jason stared at her, torn between scratching his own skin off and taking her up on her offer. Fuck, he was screwed up. He pressed the heels of his palms into his eyes.

Unexpectedly, the decision was made for him. The door flew open and light as bright as the rising sun flooded over his naked body. Soleil.

"Jason, what are you doing here?" His brother's ex-girlfriend entered the room, glowing like she'd swallowed the sun. And of course, in a way she had. Soleil, like all the women at the bordello, was celestial fae. Each had a planet or star that powered their existence. Hers was the sun itself, and the effect was extraordinary. "Do I need to call your brother?"

"No. And I'd appreciate you giving me the same privacy you provide your other patrons," he said, trying unsuccessfully to cover himself.

"My other patrons don't have a werewolf acolyte sitting in my foyer demanding to see them, with an incubus demon backup no less. He's sniffing the customers. Some of my girls can feel him drawing on their energy."

"Selene is here?"

"Indeed." Soleil handed him his pants and gave him a pitying look. "You and your money are always welcome here, Jason, but please get dressed. I'm sure you understand. The incubus is bad for business."

* * * * *

"I needed a release. You saw how dangerous my vice can be, Selene. I might've hurt you if I hadn't used the bordello." Still could hurt her. His wolf, although distracted, had yet to be appeased.

Selene didn't say a word. She entered his apartment looking tired and smelling slightly of sulfur.

"You shouldn't have gone to Lost Things. That place is dangerous. A woman like you could get hurt."

"A woman like me?"

"An acolyte. An innocent."

Selene tossed her purse on the sofa and retrieved a bottle of water from the fridge. "I'm not as helpless as you think."

"I don't think you're helpless, okay?" Jason took a seat at the table, feeling like a supreme asshole for everything that had happened that night. "I just think… what's going on with me is a little out of your league. I don't think this is going to work out. I need a different kind of therapy."

She strode toward him, leaning her hip against the side of the table, her round bottom coming tantalizingly close to the place his hand rested on the white oak top. Move his pinky an inch and he'd be touching her, feeling the firmness of her flesh taut beneath the fabric of her jeans.

"I'm here for a reason, and I don't give up easily," she said. He heard her voice as if his head were under water. He pictured his hand stroking down her stomach. A growl rumbled deep within him.

He licked his lips. His mouth had gone dry, bone dry. And her body shimmered like a cool glass of water. He squirmed under her violet stare, his gaze raking over her chest, her torso, her legs. Although it was clear she'd sensed him staring, she didn't move, didn't pull away. His wolf stood and his human body followed, rounding the table and pressing in close to her. His hands came to rest on either side of her hips.

"What are you doing?" she whispered.

"You're a beautiful woman. I know you're attracted to me. I can smell it."

"I'm here to help you. It's time to begin your therapy."

"Right. Tapping into my soul. Shouldn't we get to know each other first?" He licked his lips and lowered his face toward hers. Deep down, Jason knew he was crossing the line, but fuck if he could control himself. Her soft voice, the delicate bones of her face, everything about her was erotically female. And her innocence, that pinnacle of virtue he'd tried to avoid before, was a huge turn-on. She was untouched, an unclaimed land waiting for an explorer to plant his flag.

"Jason, this isn't…" She tried to slide out from between his arms. No way was his wolf going to go for that. His palm landed on her waist, her T-shirt bunching so that his hand touched a sliver of her skin. Heat scorched the narrow point of contact, electric sparks tingling through his arm and sending a wave of desire straight to his cock.

He lifted her bottom fully onto the table, positioning himself between her knees. She leaned away from him, her mouth working as if she wanted to say something but couldn't form the words. Bringing his nose close to her neck, he inhaled deeply. The sharp tang of her arousal was tempered ever so slightly by a whiff of fear.

"Don't fight it, Selene. It's natural. I'm a male. You're female. Just two people who need each other, taking solace from an unforgiving world in the safety of each other's arms."

"No," she said, but the word was flimsy and hollow.

"Hmm? Your words don't match the scent you're putting off, darling."

"Don't call me darling. My name is Selene." She patted herself on the chest between their bodies. "I'm

Selene, Jason. This isn't you. It's your vice. Don't let it own you."

"What's your vice, Selene?" He sniffed up her neck to her ear, so close her body heat seared his flesh. "You're trembling. What is it that you can't get enough of?"

She stilled within his arms, serenity seizing her, filling her from the bottom up. Her violet gaze snapped to his and the blush bled from her cheeks. "Helping people," she whispered. "I'm so sorry, Jason."

"Sorry for what?"

Selene's hands landed on his chest. He had a split second to notice the symbols painted on her palms, to wonder what they meant and how long they'd been there, before a shock rocked his body. His muscles seized as a hook seemed to slide between his ribs and dig into his heart. Unable to move anything but his eyes, his gaze locked on hers.

"I didn't want to have to do it this way. But you leave me no choice."

TWELVE

Selene's vision blurred, everything vibrating like a plucked chord. The walls melted away, and her spirit left her body, crossing into a dark place of spiderwebs and flashes of light. Pulses of energy flowed along strands that crisscrossed around her. Memories. Jason's memories. She was inside the core of Jason's personality, every experience tangled around her like a puzzle begging to be solved.

It was tempting to move toward the warmth coming from the light strands, but that wasn't why she was here. Oh, she'd do that eventually. Find his anchor the same way Artemis had found hers. But today, she was searching for the source of his vice, a clue to the unfulfilled need that drove his addiction. She turned toward the darkness, the cold. A black tangle at the back of the web, hidden deep within the shadows of his psyche, made her shiver with dread. This was the source, the event that turned a simple, controllable desire for sex into an unmanageable monster that ruled Jason's life. If he were to overcome his vice, he needed to face this darkness. As she approached, a chill coursed over her skin.

It was true, he might have been able to find this trigger himself given years of therapy. But he didn't have years. Whether he admitted it or not, he needed her. The faster he faced this darkness, the sooner he could walk fully in the light and the sooner he could free himself from Nickelova's hold over him.

Gently, she reached out and touched the root of the darkest thread. For a heartbeat, it felt rough between her fingers, like spun asphalt, and then she was inside the memory, standing in a college classroom.

Most of the students were human, but she spotted Jason right away next to the only other shifter Selene sensed in the room. At the front of the lecture hall, a female professor spoke. "Everything we take for granted comes from somewhere. It's a construct of our chemistry and our environment. What we consider sexual norms are simply those imposed on us by our community." Her eyes fell on Jason.

"Why is she staring at you like that?" the boy, the other shifter, whispered to Jason.

"None of your business."

"Is there something going on between you and Ms. Matthews?"

"Is there a reason you're not minding your own fucking business?" Jason's eyes darkened as he turned them on his friend.

The friend chuckled. "Dude, she's hot but she's twice your age."

"Still not your business."

The clock ticked to the hour. "Read chapter twenty for Thursday," Professor Matthews said. "Jason Flynn, I need to see you about your paper." She held up a stack of stapled assignments.

"Whatever." With a sharp look, the shifter next to Jason gathered his things and followed the others out the door.

Jason stood and descended the stairs of the emptying auditorium, Professor Matthews tapping the toe of her red pump as he neared. "I'm afraid your work isn't up to par," she said.

"I followed the rubric. Everything you asked for is there."

"Not everything."

"Tell me what's missing. I'll rewrite it."

"You know what's missing."

He swallowed, hard.

She gestured toward the door as a student entered early for the next class. "Come with me." She led him out of the lecture hall and across the building to her office. Jason's shoulders slumped, his expression like a lamb to slaughter.

Professor Matthews closed the door behind him, the lock clicking into place. "Now, show me why I should reread this paper, Jason."

He dropped his backpack on a leather chair near the window, setting his cell phone on the seat next to it. "This has to stop."

"I'll decide when it stops. Do you want me to reread the paper, or will you be taking an F?"

Looking disgusted with himself, Jason snatched the paper from her hands and slapped it down on the desk. He grabbed her by the neck and bent her over until her nose touched the printed sheets.

"No better time than the present," he said. The hand that wasn't holding her neck down hitched her skirt up to her waist and unfastened his fly. With a snap, he tore her panties from her hips and tossed them into the garbage bin near her desk. The woman moaned.

"This is the last time," Jason said through his teeth. "It's over."

She grinned over her shoulder. "It's over when I decide it is."

He entered her roughly, still fully dressed, his hand moving from her neck to her mouth as her moans became loud enough to be heard through the walls. This wasn't lovemaking; it was sex—brutal, punishing sex that made Selene wish she could look away. Jason's eyes were dead, his hips thrusting like a machine. After several torturous minutes, Ms. Matthews's body twitched under him, the force of her orgasm evident in the contortion of her limbs.

Jason pulled out and came down the back of her legs.

Professor Matthews rocked on the desk, her hips rolling, but Jason backed away like the very sight of her disgusted him. He zipped his pants and picked up his backpack, staring at the door while she composed herself. She flashed him a wicked smile.

"A-plus," she said, holding up the paper. "You're a natural."

Jason scowled, refusing to look at her. "Can I go?" Selene noticed a number of missed messages flashing across the screen of his phone, now cradled in his hand like a talisman against evil. They were from Silas. His brother had been trying to reach him.

Ms. Matthews gripped Jason's lower jaw and forced him to look at her. "Such a pretty face. Don't feel guilty about this, darling. We're just two people taking solace from an unforgiving world in the safety of each other's arms."

"There's only one person here whose grades are at stake."

"Hey, you signed up for this. Do I need to remind you—"

"No. I remember."

"Then, I'll see you next… assignment." Jason unlocked the door and let himself out.

The scene faded, and so did Selene. She came out of his memories, exhausted and feeling filthy. It took her a moment to reorient herself. She was perched on the table next to Jason's kitchen, his awake but unresponsive body between her thighs. Promptly, she removed her hands from his chest to halt the ritual.

And watched him collapse on the floor near her feet.

* * * * *

Jason hit the floor and rolled onto his back. Everything hurt as if Selene had reached down his throat, grabbed his intestines, and wrapped them around the bumper of a moving bus. He curled on his side and heaved. There was nothing inside him to come out. Truly nothing. He felt like an empty husk.

"Just lie still," Selene said softly. "You'll be all right. You just need rest."

He couldn't have responded if he'd wanted to. His body shivered uncontrollably, his teeth chattering, and every sweat gland in his body seemed to open at once. The front of his shirt quickly soaked through.

She pressed two fingers against his neck and frowned. "Let's get you into bed."

Hooking her hands under his armpits, she dragged him into the bedroom and lifted him onto the bed, a feat that wouldn't have been possible had she not been a werewolf. His muscles were useless, twitching things. He couldn't help her or fight her.

She unbuttoned his wet shirt and rolled him out of it. There was nothing sexual about the act. If anything, it was humiliating, although he was too tired to register that particular emotion. He blinked, and she was gone.

When he opened his eyes again, Selene was wringing a washcloth in a basin. She lifted one of his arms and scrubbed. She rinsed it out again. Jason closed his eyes.

He opened them again and he was in his pajamas. She was there, sitting by his bed, watching him. She'd changed her clothes. He closed his eyes again.

"Time to eat," she said. She was holding him up, spooning soup into his mouth. She'd changed her clothes again. This time she looked worried. He glanced at his useless hands and noticed symbols painted on his palms. He was too weak to ask why they were there. He closed his eyes again.

She was rolling him over. He blinked and rubbed his face. He heard her exhale in relief. "Thank the goddess." He closed his eyes again.

"Jason? Jason." Selene's short, natural nails shook his shoulder, just below his Fireborn tattoo.

"Haven't you had enough, darling?" he asked, laughing to himself.

"Why is that funny? And don't call me darling. It's Selene."

He rolled over and looked at her, his face falling. "What have you done to me?"

She hesitated. "Do you think you can make it to the bathtub? I've filled it for you and I'd like you to try to get up. You've been ill."

He tested his arms and legs, then nodded.

Sitting him up, she swung his legs off the bed and helped him plant his feet. After a few false starts, she looped his arm around her shoulders and helped him to his feet. Step by step they made their way to the bathroom where she undressed him like a child. She helped him step into the tub and lowered him into the water.

"You had a fever," she said. "A high fever. But it's over now."

"…Kill me," he mumbled.

"No. I'm not going to kill you. It's going to be okay."

He shook his head. "You tried to kill me," he said more clearly.

She sighed. "No. I did what I needed to do to start your recovery. I didn't want to hurt you. We were supposed to do that gently, from a relaxed, seated position. In an ideal world, you would have let me in. But you forced my hand when you threatened me."

Jason laid his head back on the side of the tub. "You could have just asked me to stop."

"I did."

He tried to think back, but all he remembered was the wolf, the overwhelming feeling of wanting her. Everything else was a blur, flashes and random images he could barely associate with the woman in front of him. He raised his wet hands to his face.

"I forgive you," Selene said. "Don't waste a second of your recovery thinking about it. I knew what I was getting myself into."

He snorted, rolling his head to the side to give her a pointed glare. "Funny, it seems I didn't."

"As long as you continue to deny you have a problem, everything we do together is going to feel like a fight, and you're the one who will wear the bruises," she said firmly.

With his eyes tightly closed, Jason asked, "Did you find what you needed? Or did you almost kill me for nothing?"

Selene sat cross-legged on the bathroom floor. "I want to talk about Professor Matthews."

The water splashed as Jason opened his eyes and unsuccessfully tried to sit up. "That's what you decided to dig out of my head? Jill Matthews?"

"She was your trigger. You keep her in the darkest corner of your mind."

He sighed. "If there was one thing Jill had in spades, it was darkness."

"I watched her take advantage of you. It was obvious you didn't want to be there but she mentioned you… signed up for something."

He leaned his head back again. He remembered but it wasn't something he liked to talk about. And it had absolutely nothing to do with his vice.

"She said the same thing to you as you said to me. 'We're just two people—'"

"'Taking solace from an unforgiving world in the safety of each other's arms.' I forgot that was something Jill used to say."

"I think it's significant."

"It was a long time ago, long before my vice was a problem."

Selene said nothing, the silence growing weighted between them.

"I'd done it before."

"Done what?"

"Slept with a teacher. The first one was named Bethany Vale. I met her at a bar before I knew who she was. We were close in age and things just happened. It had nothing to do with grades. But Professor Matthews found out. She said she'd tell the dean, have Bethany fired. I cared for her. It wasn't just sex. Then Jill said there was another way."

"You agreed to give her what she wanted in exchange for her silence," Selene whispered.

Jason nodded slowly.

"She used you."

"Until someone younger and more interesting came along."

"So, that's what started it."

"No." Jason shook his head. "My vice was there after the first time I shifted, and it was relatively mild until…"

"Until that day. I saw you in her office. Silas was trying to call you."

The scene that played out in Jason's head made his stomach turn again and a wave of exhaustion overcame him. He closed his eyes. "I don't want to talk about this."

"Why was Silas calling you that day?" She lowered herself to her knees next to the tub and folded her arms on the edge, nothing but compassion in her voice.

"Can we take a break? Plenty of time to probe my subconscious and torture me with the results later, right?" He looked at his hands in the water. The symbols she'd drawn there had washed away and turned the bath slightly red.

She didn't waver from her goal. "Why was Silas calling you?"

"I… I'm naked. Can you hand me a towel?"

Selene raised her eyebrows and smiled roguishly. "You weren't wearing one when I put you in there."

"Hide your virgin eyes, woman!" he tried to tease. "Aren't you supposed to maintain your innocence? One look at my member and you'll be ruined for celibacy."

The corner of her mouth twitched up. "Sorry to break it to you, but I had more than an eyeful when I was in your memories, not to mention while I was taking care of you over the last four days. I think I can control myself."

"Four days?" Jason wiped a hand over his face.

She nodded slowly. "By the way, acolytes are celibate—they're not necessarily virgins."

Jason lifted an eyebrow. "Pass the popcorn, someone has a story to tell. What in the goddess's name are you saying?"

"Tell me why Silas was calling and I'll get you out of this tub and tell you my story."

He took a deep breath and watched a bead of water roll down the tiled wall. There was no getting around this. She wasn't going to let it drop. "Silas was calling to tell me... my parents had been shot. He called to tell me they were dead. Alex Bloodright shot my parents while I was fucking Jill Matthews."

THIRTEEN

"Which drawer?" Selene drifted to his dresser.

"Third on the left," Jason said. He was sitting naked on the bed, and by the way he swayed, having a hard time remaining upright.

"It's okay if you want to lie down," she said as she retrieved a pair of sweats and a T-shirt.

When she turned back around, he was scowling at her. "Doesn't it bother your acolyte-ness to see me naked?"

"Like I said, most of us had lives before we joined the order. I joined at sixteen. I've seen a dick before."

Jason broke out in a fit of coughing, staring at her as if deeply disturbed by her use of the word *dick*. Well, he could think what he wanted to. She had no intention of deceiving him into believing she was somehow better than anyone else. Selene had a past, and if Jason knew that, it might give him the hope that he too could overcome his.

She pulled his T-shirt over his head and knelt in front of him to help him into his sweats. Her cheeks grew warm when she found herself eye to eye with the male member they'd just been discussing. Nothing about Jason was average or unattractive. She stood up, trying her best to hide her body's response to him. He finished pulling them on himself.

"Are you okay?" he said, with an impish smile. "You're flushed."

Rolling her eyes, she wiped the back of her hand across her sweating forehead. This would be so much easier if Jason were old or plain or smelled differently. Oh goddess, she loved his smell, an earthy concoction of warm cloves and ground chicory that seemed to ooze naturally from his pores. She looked away for a moment.

"I need something to eat and I know you do too. Can you make it to the kitchen, or do you want me to bring you something in here?"

"I can make it… with your help." He held out a hand to her. She helped him up and they slowly made their way into the great room, where she propped him in a chair at the dining table. As she moved into the kitchen to start lunch, his silence surprised her. He gave her nothing. No teasing. No insults. No anger.

She'd almost finished frying up a couple of hamburgers when he finally spoke.

"I've spent a long time trying to forget that day," he said.

Selene didn't say anything, just glanced at him and plated the burgers, adding chips along the edge of the plate.

"You must think I'm trash. Royal trash. Nothing but a waste of oxygen."

Her face tightened and she moved the food to the table. She stared at Jason for a moment, then placed her hands on either side of his face. "Being used by someone does not make you trash. Jill Matthews is trash."

"And I'm worse?" Dark circles had appeared under his eyes. He was coming apart.

"No. You're extraordinary. Because you are going to survive this. You are going to overcome what she did to you. And I'm going to celebrate every baby step while you do." She searched his eyes.

For a moment, she was staring straight into his soul, at a boy who'd hidden so much pain for so long that he didn't know what to do with it now that it was exposed. But like a switch, she watched him change. He camouflaged his despair with a thick blanket of cynicism and that roguish grin that tugged somewhere deep inside her. She slid a hamburger in front of him.

"You owe me a story," he said. "Of how you're not a virgin."

She retrieved two teacups and filled them both with the hot tea she'd made while he was sleeping. Waves of steam twisted from the surface, the scent of lemon and orange blossom filling her nostrils. She didn't want to talk about this with him. She'd promised in the heat of the moment, but now she regretted the offer.

"You should eat something," she said.

To her relief, Jason began to eat in earnest, although he searched her face as if trying to decipher her expression. "What made you decide to become an acolyte?" he asked between bites.

Selene took a long sip of tea and thought about the question. Should she answer it honestly or give him the sanitized version she used in polite conversation? She looked at him over the lip of her teacup. Sweat was visible on his upper lip and every time he lifted the burger to his mouth his hands shook so hard the sandwich began to come apart. She pushed her plate across the table and moved beside him, rather than across from him.

"Can I help you with that?" She reached for the burger.

He shook his head. "I can feed myself."

"I'll tell you what, if you allow me to help you, I'll tell you the story of how I became an acolyte."

His eyes narrowed but he seemed to have no fight left in him to argue. With a deep sigh, he gave her one curt nod.

"I wasn't always a member of Fireborn pack." She cut the burger into quarters and raised one to his lips, trying not to think of how intimate the gesture felt.

"I was wondering. I don't remember you as a child or a teen but then my family…"

"Royalty is often separated from the masses." She lifted the sleeve of her T-shirt to reveal her pack tattoo. "I didn't become a Fireborn until I was sixteen. I believe you were already at university by then."

"What pack were you with before?" Jason asked, taking another bite from her fingers.

Selene shook her head. "Running solo."

Jason arched an eyebrow. "No pack at all?"

"I was born into a human family. Both human. The first time I shifted, my father tried to shoot me. I didn't remember, of course. I was fifteen and had a fever. The heat was so extreme I became delirious and stumbled outside into the snow in the middle of the night. I woke up the next morning, naked, shivering, with blood on my face. After I snuck back into the house, my father told my mother that he'd shot at a wolf hanging around our front porch. I didn't know that wolf was me. Not yet."

"You're lucky to be alive. Most werewolves born to human parents don't make it through the first shift."

"I wasn't a genetic anomaly. My mother recognized the signs and told me what I was. The man I thought was my father, wasn't. My mother became pregnant by a werewolf and pawned me off on my human father when the guy hit the road. She didn't even remember his full name."

"Oh, Selene." Jason shook his head.

"The next time I shifted, I did it where both my parents could see. I thought if I brought it out in the open, things would be different. I thought they'd help me. The next day, I left for school. When I came back, they were gone."

"Gone?"

"They moved." Her gaze drifted toward the window. "While I was in class, so that they wouldn't have to face me, the only family I'd ever known abandoned me."

"What happened to you? How did you survive?"

"The landlord kicked me out of the house soon after. I lived on the street for a while. Did things I'm not proud of to survive. Stole. Hurt people." She frowned at her plate. "And other things. Whatever I had to do."

Jason's face went slack. He stared at her like he'd never seen her before.

"At first, I had this dream that my real father might find me. But eventually, I gave up on that idea. I'd shift alone and always shift back alone. And then one day, a man was there when I shifted back. He insisted I come with him to Rivergate. He introduced me to Artemis, and she took me under her wing. The rest is, as they say, history."

"Who was the man?"

Selene smiled. "Your brother Silas. He'd been out working a case and shifted outside the grounds. His wolf found me."

"Silas." Jason stared absently straight ahead.

"Well, after that happened, Artemis asked me to join Fireborn since I had no claim to any pack. I accepted and decided soon after that I wanted to be just like Artemis. Besides your brother, she is the only person on this earth I ever fully trusted. The only one I do trust with my life and my soul."

Jason gave her a pitying glance. "You've had a rough start."

"It made me value relationships and the role of the goddess in our lives. Finding a home with Fireborn pack made me believe I was destined to follow in Artemis's footsteps."

"You aspire to be the pack priestess."

"All acolytes do."

"Some more than others." He tilted his head.

"There are some who quit early on, but I've been doing this for almost three years now and it's the first time I've felt fully connected to anything. Artemis thinks I may be the one to take over her role when she retires."

Jason selected another piece of burger and successfully brought it to his mouth.

"You're doing better. I told you that you were hungry."

"Can I ask you something?"

"Something else? I feel like I'm giving you my life history."

"You said I wasn't the first man you'd seen naked."

"You're not."

"When you say you did things to survive…"

Selene sighed. He was going to make her say it. "I had sex in exchange for things, to survive. Sometimes by choice. Sometimes by force. Never a good experience. I don't like to talk about it."

Jason growled.

"It was a long time ago." She lowered her chin and stared at him.

His brows knit, and he shook his head. "I'm sorry, Selene. I almost forced myself on you the other night. I was out of control. It must have been terrifying, especially considering your past." He leaned toward her, his gaze locking with hers. "I'd never hurt you. Not intentionally."

For a long time, she simply stared at him, sizing him up. "I know." Her voice was barely audible. She picked at her food. "Now, I've answered your questions. You need to answer mine."

"I thought I did. What other questions could you have?"

"What was it about Ms. Matthews—"

"That allowed her to fuel the darkest part of me?"

Selene nodded. "I feel like I don't have the full story."

Jason glanced toward the balcony. "Come outside with me?"

"Jason…"

"I'll tell you. Just help me outside. If I eat another bite I'm going to pop. I haven't seen the sun in four days."

She stood and helped him to the balcony. A warm breeze circled her shoulders as she lowered Jason onto one of the sling-back chairs.

"Do you want me to get you a blanket?" she asked.

"No. I'm okay."

Selene sat down beside him, trying to be patient.

"Considering she was a human, Professor Matthews had quite the appetite. Once or twice a week she'd call me into her office and I'd do what I thought I had to do. Until during one session, my phone rang. I didn't answer it, not until later when I was back at my dorm room."

"Who was it?" Selene's voice felt thin and weak.

"It was my mom. She wanted to talk to me about a charity performance she was going to with my father. My parents had invited my siblings and me to go as well, but I couldn't because of Professor Matthews. My sister couldn't go either because she was finishing an intense veterinary medicine program at the time. And Silas couldn't go because he was a new detective and he was working that night." Jason's voice petered out at the end until she could barely hear him. She threaded her fingers into his and squeezed.

"It's understandable, Jason."

He turned his head to look at her, his green eyes as cutting and bright as emeralds. "My parents were gunned down in the Harlequin Theater at that performance. That call and that message were the last time I heard my mother's voice. Not only did I miss Silas's call weeks later to tell me they were dead, but I missed my last chance to talk to them while they were still alive. I never called my mother back. I was ashamed. I didn't want to talk to her in case something in my voice gave away what I was doing with Jill. All because I couldn't say no. I couldn't face the consequences of my actions."

Selene's lips parted and she took a tiny sip of air, trying her best not to react to the revelation, not to feel the aching pain that rolled off Jason like a fog and settled right over her heart. The look on his face said it all. He loathed himself. Loathed what he'd done.

Standing from her chair, Selene knelt in front of him on the concrete, placing her hands on top of his.

"You couldn't have known what would happen. It isn't your fault."

"No? Maybe if I'd had a spine. If I'd stood up to her… maybe I would have gone with my parents to that stupid play, and maybe I could have stopped Alex."

"Maybe. Or you might have been another of his victims. Your mother knew you loved her. If she were here, she'd tell you she forgives you for that day and many others. She'd want you to forgive yourself."

"How do you know?" Jason's green eyes were wet with unshed tears.

"I'm an acolyte, Jason." Selene squeezed his hands. "Goddess willing, it's my job to know."

FOURTEEN

Jason's head pounded like the drum line in a subpar marching band. He'd hoped he could work a little, knew that after four days his inbox would be full, but after staring at a single e-mail for the better part of an hour, he conceded he wasn't ready.

Shuffling from his room, he found Selene curled in the leather chair with one of the few magazines he kept in the apartment, *The Economist*. Her violet eyes stared past the page with the sort of intense boredom you might see at a daylong insurance seminar.

"How about a movie?" Jason asked.

"Please." She closed the magazine. "If you're not too tired. It's getting late."

"I've spent days in bed." He grimaced. "I have no desire to go back there. Not yet."

"What do you want to watch?"

"The DVDs are inside the cabinet to the right of the fireplace. If you don't see anything you like, we can download something."

She crossed the room and popped open the cabinet. He watched her sit cross-legged on the floor like a child, perusing each title. What would she pick? He kept a number of romantic titles for his female guests, but there were a few in there he actually liked.

"Here we go." She pulled a disc from the case and slid it into the machine.

Jason smiled. She'd chosen his favorite. "*The Lord of the Rings*? A strange choice for an acolyte."

"What do you think acolytes should watch?"

"*The Sound of Music*," Jason responded immediately.

Selene's mouth dropped open. "You do understand I don't make my own clothes from my curtains."

He eyed her jeans and T-shirt combo. "You paid for that?"

"Not everyone needs or can afford monogrammed dress shirts, *Prince* Jason." She stood from the floor and flopped onto the oatmeal couch. He crossed the room to sit down beside her.

"You're a beautiful woman. Maybe I need to make a donation to Sanctuary. Artemis needs to take better care of her acolytes." Jason sat down beside her.

Her body tensed. Perhaps she was remembering the way he'd thrown her against the wall. Jason was probably like a dark cave to her. Once you'd seen the bear go in, even if you never saw it again, you'd never trust the darkness. You'd assume the bear was in there, hiding in the shadows.

She scooted away from him, closer to the armrest. "How are you feeling?"

Jason leaned his head back and analyzed her body language. Yep, she was afraid. Goddess, he owed her one. "My wolf is still making demands, but he's not as loud inside my head as he used to be. Actually, when I think about what I did to you, it makes me feel ill. It was uncalled for. It won't happen again."

Selene glanced at her fingers tangled in her lap. "Then we accomplished our goal. You've seen your vice for what it is."

"So, that's it? I'm cured?"

She snorted. "No. Not yet. Your vice will grow stronger with time, but the more you practice pushing it away, the longer it will stay away."

"What's next then? To cure me?" he asked.

"I'll teach you coping techniques—meditation, anchoring—so when it does happen, you'll be ready. You can do this, Jason. The hardest part is over."

"Thank you." His eyes met hers. All he could think was that she was the most beautiful woman he'd ever known. Not sexy, but beautiful, down to her very soul.

"You're welcome."

Jason leaned back against the sofa and for the first time in forever, he felt truly *with* a woman. As he glanced over at her, taking her in while she watched the movie, his chest swelled with respect and admiration. When this was all over, he hoped they'd stay friends, even after she became a priestess.

"Jason?" She turned and his heart leapt when her gaze fell on him.

"Yes?"

"This is the most uncomfortable couch I've ever sat on." She shifted awkwardly.

"Admittedly." He chuckled.

"It feels like I'm sitting on a burlap bag full of ball bearings."

"Completely uncomfortable." He nodded.

She spread her hands in confusion. "Why do you own this?"

He shrugged. "Someone told me it was the best."

"Someone lied to you." She started laughing. "Never trust that person again."

He was laughing with her when his phone rang. "I've got to take this." She nodded as he rose and scrambled from the couch, jogging out onto the balcony for some privacy. As he watched Selene through the glass door, he answered the call.

"Hey, sexy. It's Thursday night and I haven't heard from you. Are you stopping by later?"

"Sarah," Jason said. "No, I can't make it tonight."

There was silence on the other end of the line. "Is this because I wouldn't go to your sister's wedding?"

"No. I'm just not… well," he said.

"Do you want me to come to your place?"

"No," Jason said too loudly. "I'm sorry, Sarah. Not tonight."

She scoffed. "What's going on? You have not missed a session with me in two years. What gives?"

Somewhere above him, a bird flapped its wings as it landed on the roof. Jason stared at it, admiring the flight, the freedom. "I've just decided you were right. I need more. I am looking for something, and what you and I had… it wasn't helping either of us."

The call went quiet except for her shuddering breath.

"Sarah, I…"

"Good luck finding whatever you're after," she said. The call ended.

Jason watched Selene through the glass, smiling as she slid from the uncomfortable couch to sit on the floor. For the hundredth time that day, he wished that things could be different, that she wasn't an acolyte, and that he didn't have a vice.

His phone call was over but he didn't rush to go back in. Instead, he rested his head against the window and just watched her.

* * * * *

Selene was curious about what was taking Jason so long on the phone. She supposed it was work related. He had been unconscious for most of four days. When he finally did return, he didn't bother with the sofa but sat down beside her on the floor. His hand landed on the carpet mere centimeters from hers, the outside of her pinky warming from the heat coming off his golden flesh. Her pulse should not have quickened, and her attention should not have lingered on the way his dark hair curved along his temple, accentuating the hard angles of his jaw.

No, she should have been afraid, afraid his wolf could smell the arousal she was suppressing. Afraid he'd break his resolve and push her against the arm of the couch the same way he'd pushed her against the wall. But that wasn't what she was afraid of. Her true fear, the one that lingered deep within, the one she'd toppled the bookcases and furniture of her mind to stop from reaching her, was that she wanted him to do it again. The memory of his body on hers and the thought that he *could* want only her were ideas so erotic they held a seductive power strong enough to make her temporarily forget her goal to become priestess.

His nostrils flared, but he didn't look at her. He watched, unblinking, as Frodo pressed his hobbit-back into the dirty nook under the road and closed his eyes against the temptation to put on the ring, even as the Ringwraith hovered over his head.

Selene pulled her hand into her lap.

FIFTEEN

"Stop fidgeting," Selene said, glancing at Jason. The east-facing balcony was bathed in the warming light of sunrise but the calming effect of the blue skies and singing birds above seemed lost on him. His face gleamed with fresh sweat and he squirmed on the yoga mat as if he were sitting on a bed of nails.

A few days had passed since she'd found his trigger. He was stronger now. He could handle more. But the wolf was back this morning with a vengeance.

They'd been experimenting with intense exercise to work off the extra physical energy related to his vice, making use of his home gym several hours a day. But all the push-ups and miles on the treadmill hadn't seemed to placate Jason's wolf today. Clearly, he wanted sex. His entire body seemed to protest for it. Selene needed to find another way to help him.

"How is this supposed to work again?" he asked.

"Take a deep breath, close your eyes, and begin the mantra I taught you. Let it pull you down into deep meditation. It will help with your withdrawal symptoms."

His shoulders slumped, his presence heavy beside her. "Every time I close my eyes, I see…"

"You see what?"

"I see myself attacking you, grabbing you by the throat, pushing you against the wall."

Selene glanced toward the door. "Now? You're fantasizing about this now?"

"No! I'm not fantasizing. I'm ashamed. That night, when I forced you to let me go to the bordello… You don't want to be here any more than I do. You certainly don't want my disgusting hands all over your body. *Fuck.*" He scrubbed his face, turning slightly away from her. "You don't understand. I couldn't help myself. What if I lose control again?"

There was a long stretch of silence. "Jason… Jason, look at me." She reached over and tugged his chin so that he faced her, although his gaze remained focused on a segment of the balcony railing over her right shoulder. "When I took this assignment, I expected that your vice would take control at some point. I was prepared. You're dealing with intense withdrawal. It's to be expected."

"No." He shook his head. "I'm dangerous. I liked the feel of you against me. My skin is crawling with need." He pushed off the mat and paced to the other side of the balcony. "What if it happens again and I can't stop? After what you've been through in your past…" He shook his head.

"My past is in my past. You are not a part of that." It was true that part of her still feared Jason on some level, and on an even deeper level, some part of her had enjoyed his touch. Saying either of those things out loud, however, wouldn't help him get better or earn her a promotion to *Preotka*. She had to stay objective. "You know firsthand that I can defend myself. I knocked you on your ass for four days."

"Yes."

"Literally knocked you into tomorrow."

"Yes."

"I can do it again."

"Please don't."

"The important thing is you didn't try to slit my throat when you woke up. You were barely angry with me."

"What good would it do to be angry at you for defending yourself from…" He pointed his hands at himself.

"That means, on some level you want to get better. You understand what we're doing here and want to succeed."

"Or I just feel disgusting for throwing myself at you."

She moistened her lips. "You're not disgusting," she said. "You have a problem and we're fixing it. That's all. You won't hurt me."

A storm moved in behind Jason's eyes, the color of his irises flashing from green to amber. He clung to the railing behind him with a white-knuckled death grip as if it were the only thing keeping him from attacking her. The darkness was back. He was a predator again.

"You don't know what you do to me. Even now, I want to slide inside you, Selene. I want to feel the heat of your skin on my tongue. I want to run my hand up the inside of your thigh." He looked her straight in the eye, and he seemed taller than a moment before. The intensity of his stare made her shiver. "Don't tell me it's okay. Tell me you understand the risks of being here and that you forgive me for wanting you."

Chest tight, Selene held his gaze. She hoped the mild breeze masked her arousal as the images he painted in her brain quickened her breath. "I… I forgive you," she said. "And I know it could happen again… but I don't think it will. You can control this. What I'm teaching you today will help."

For a long time, he simply stared at her, breathing. Slowly, his amber eyes turned green again. He lowered himself to the mat, crossed his legs, and straightened his spine.

"Close your eyes," she said quietly. He did.

With a deep, cleansing breath, Selene centered herself. "Let's try again."

This time Jason got it right. The space beside her grew quiet and cool. His fidgeting stopped. Her ears lost the thump of his racing heart. But he'd need help to go deeper, to that place of healing she knew he must go. That's where she came in.

Closing her eyes, she threaded her fingers into his, ignoring the way the touch of his hand sent a warm current of heat up her arm. He must have felt it too because his body stiffened. She began her mantra.

Meditation was a grounding force in Selene's life, a way of centering herself that had saved her from the shame of being homeless and the shame of all the things she'd done to survive. It had helped her transition into the order and strengthened her mind. Desperately, she wanted to give Jason this tool to ease the suffering she'd seen in him. She reached out from her center, psychically surrounded him, and lowered him into that space between sleep and awake.

In that wide-open consciousness, color, emotion, and pure mindfulness were all that existed. The muddy-green color of his aura became palpable, clouding the pale blue of her own. Jason's aura was dark, but at the heart of it, a spark of bright green burned, crystal clear and lit from within. This was what she was trying to save. This was Jason. The real Jason.

She gripped his hand tighter, her bright blue light coming to rest next to his bright green one. And that's where she stayed. There was nothing sexual about the encounter, but there could be nothing more intimate. Her soul rested with his in a place beyond time or space. They revolved around each other, two stars orbiting, held in the other's gravitational pull.

When it was time to kick off the bottom and float back to the real world, Selene had to do the kicking. She'd practiced this. It would take Jason time to learn to go this deep and know when it was time to come back to reality.

A deep breath drew into her lungs as she broke the surface. But when she turned to check on Jason, her breath hitched in her throat. His face was serene, all the fear, longing, and bitterness his body had held only moments ago replaced by a deep peace. He'd even stopped sweating.

She opened her hand, releasing his fingers. No tremors. No pain. No wanting. The muscles of his jaw were relaxed. She almost hated to bring him out of it, but the beneficial effects would diminish if he stayed where he was. Softly, she whispered his name, "Jason."

* * * * *

He was safe. Safe and warm and cared for. There was no endless wanting, no bottomless pit of shame or ache of need. And the source of this serenity was in his hand, nestled between his fingers. Then it was gone.

Desperate to return to that place of peace, he tried to reach for the hand again. But she denied him. He opened his eyes. There was an angel hovering over him, a bright blue angel with the sunrise spilling through a curtain of her hair like liquid gold. For a moment, he lost himself in the connection they shared. Pure light poured into his heart and filled him. He wasn't alone.

"Welcome back," the angel said. Selene. Her name was Selene.

And then the blue faded and his hands began to shake again. His mouth went as dry as a stone. A muscle in his leg cramped to the point of pain, and a hardcore throb began between his temples as if a little man was building a railroad between his eyes.

"I need a drink."

"How about an aspirin?" She held out her hand to help him up.

The corner of his mouth lifted and he shook his head. "I think I'd better get up on my own." He avoided her touch as he stood.

She sighed and let him go.

* * * * *

Weeks later, Jason woke, knowing the full moon was just around the corner. It was a good thing he'd made slow and steady progress with Selene's help, because his wolf would be close to the surface today. In two days, he'd have to endure the shift and face dozens of women he'd slept with at Rivergate. He'd thrown himself into his therapy with the same determination and fortitude he'd always devoted to his business. And he was healing. Controlling himself around Selene was getting easier, despite wanting her every minute of the day. They'd fallen into a kind of routine, a routine he could get used to.

This morning, as usual, he drifted to the coffee machine while Selene started chopping vegetables for omelets. He'd just filled the water reservoir when she said something that chilled him to the bone. "I think we should try aura manipulation again today."

Aura manipulation. That's what she'd done to him before, the thing that had almost killed him. His neck craned and his eyes locked onto hers. "Why? I thought you found the source of my vice the first time. If there's something more, I sure as hell don't know what it is."

"My first time in your psyche, I was looking for the source of the darkness within you. This time, I want to look for the source of the light, an anchor you can hold onto if you feel like you might lose control. If you become aware of what strengthens your soul and you foster it, Nickelova's curse won't be able to take root in you. If she comes back, she won't be able to control you."

He switched on the coffee pot, then realized he'd forgotten to add coffee and switched it back off. As he pulled the ground beans from the pantry, he asked, "What if you can't find any light in me? What if you drift down my lightbulb aisle and find nothing but an assortment of coal and cinders?"

She snorted. "You have light. I saw it while we were meditating. I just couldn't see the source. It's bright green. Your soul is beautiful."

Jason stared at her for a moment. "Is yours blue?"

She nodded excitedly. "Yes! Yes. You saw it? That's really good, Jason. The scrolls say that if you can sense someone's aura you're in the presence of the goddess herself. That type of meditation is as good as a prayer."

"The goddess, huh." He took a deep breath. "I never actually believed in the goddess. I'm still not sure there isn't another explanation for what you do."

"How do you explain how I saved you from the curse? I'm not a witch. My only power comes from my connection to the goddess through our religious order."

His brow furrowed. "How *did* you lift my curse?"

"I didn't lift it, exactly. I performed a ritual asking the goddess to transfer it into me." She pointed at her chest.

"Then why aren't you catatonic in bed like I was?"

"My training and lifestyle keep me pure. Nickelova's curse was attached to your vice, but when I transferred it into me, there was no place for it to take root. It fizzled and died like a seed on concrete."

"Your innocence saved you."

"I told you last night, I'm not exactly innocent, but my way of life is powerful."

"Virtue is powerful," he murmured more to himself than to her. It had been a long time since he'd thought of the goddess or his place in the universe. What was it about Selene? Every moment he spent with her challenged him to be a better person. "Thank you for risking yourself for me."

Selene blushed and turned toward the frying pan.

"Are you all right? Did I say something wrong?"

She plated the eggs. "Just fine. Let's eat. I want to get started as soon as possible."

SIXTEEN

To say that Jason was apprehensive about Selene entering his memories again was an understatement. The first time had felt like having his heart pulled out of his nostril, chewed up, and spit back into the opposite nostril. Silas had been right. The woman sitting cross-legged before him looked as sweet and gentle as an angel, but the power in those dainty, tapered fingers, those two hands adorned with ritualistic symbols, was as fierce and powerful as the goddess's.

"You're trembling again," Selene said. "Are the withdrawal symptoms coming back?"

"No."

"Then what's wrong?"

"I'm scared shitless. I don't want to end up in bed for four days again."

She took one of his hands in hers, and Jason had to suppress the temptation to pull her forward the extra inch and press his lips to hers. "Trust me, Jason. Last time I was rough with you. I had to be. You were fighting me at every turn. This time, it won't be like that. You know why we're doing this now. You've already come so far. Open yourself up to me."

He nodded. What other choice did he have? Her hand on his might as well have been a steel binding. His heart would have skipped out of his chest and slid down his arm to be part of that coupling, the traitor.

"The only way to conquer a vice is to discover the need it's trying to fill and fill it with something else. Today, I'm going to find a memory of something that once filled that need, before your vice took hold. One so bright and powerful it will become an anchor, holding you to your true need, keeping you from floating too far toward your vice."

"Okay. Why can't I remember it on my own?"

"Believe it or not, our minds have a way of shielding us from the good as well as the bad. I'll be able to remind you of things you may not recall on your own." Adjusting herself so that her knees touched his, she moved her hands to hover over his heart. "Ready?"

"Yes," he said. He wasn't ready. Not really. But he trusted her.

She closed her eyes and gently touched his chest.

* * * * *

At the moment her hands touched Jason's chest, Selene felt the familiar shifting as if the rate of the earth revolving on its axis increased threefold. The great room melted away and she stood in the infinite web of pulsing strands that made up his memories. With a jolt, she noticed the dark tangle she'd visited before, the memory of Professor Matthews was lighter in color now, the strands still coiled tightly but not tied in knots like before. He'd accepted the events and was starting to heal emotionally. Good.

She scanned the web looking for the light. Bright green pulsed above her and she followed it toward a particularly bright spot in his consciousness.

But when she found the brightest, warmest spot in his memories, she had trouble reaching it. It was all tangled up and hidden by dark sections so that she almost couldn't tell where the light began and the darkness ended. Reaching out, she folded her hand to navigate the knot until, with surgical precision, her fingers slid over the argent thread at its center. Blinding light surrounded her, transported her, and she found herself standing in a kitchen.

The smell of baking gingerbread cookies filled her nostrils and the laughter of three teenage siblings met her ears. She knew these kids. The royal family: Silas, Jason, and Laina. Which meant that the woman swaying and humming in front of the stove was their mother. A white candle inside a glass hurricane lamp burned brightly between them, surrounded by an arrangement of greens, red berries, and ribbon. *Christmas,* she thought.

"You should take French, Jason. The girls love a man who can speak French," Silas said. He looked to be eighteen or nineteen and was wearing a Cornell T-shirt.

"Silas," the dark-haired girl said, rolling her eyes. Laina. "Jason shouldn't choose a language to study based on its ability to woo girls. He should be thinking about college and employment opportunities." Laina rubbed the youngest boy's shoulders. "Study Spanish or, better yet, Mandarin."

Their mother left the stove to plant a kiss on the side of Jason's head. "Choose what speaks to your heart. If you follow your passion, the universe will find the right place for you." She ruffled his hair before crossing back to the stove to pull the tray of cookies from the oven.

"Mom, that's terrible advice!" Laina said. "Who knows what stupid ideas his heart will come up with? He could end up wasting his time on something utterly useless, like… like Italian."

A lanky man with glasses and a hint of gray in his hair strode in and spun Mrs. Flynn around. "*Cosa c'è di sbagliato con l'italiano?*"

Mrs. Flynn looked up into her husband's eyes and adjusted her arms around his neck. She took a deep, contented breath. "Personally, I love Italian," she whispered into her husband's lips. The two parents danced between the oven and the kitchen island, drawn into each other as if they were the only two people on the planet.

Silas groaned. "Ugh! Get a room." He cupped a hand over his eyes and exchanged awkward glances with his siblings.

"I have a room," Mr. Flynn said through a barely restrained smile. "I have an entire house. You just happen to live in it." They broke into laughter as he spun Mrs. Flynn from his arms.

After a short peck on her husband's cheek, she grabbed the tray of cookies and slid them onto the island. "Who's ready for gingerbread?"

The three teens popped up and Jason pried a cookie from the tray with his bare fingers, tossing it between his hands to keep them from burning. His face… Selene couldn't look away. He was so open, so innocent, so trusting. But the predominant feeling, as she stood in this memory, was love. Unconditional love. Familial love.

This was it. This was his anchor.

As the memory ended, Selene experienced the familiar rushing fall of her extraction from his consciousness with mixed emotions. She desperately wanted to stay in that kitchen, in that safe place of love and warmth, but it wasn't her life or her memory. It was Jason's. Her job was to share it with him, to remind him of the place of love that he came from, the thing he could cling to when the darkness was close at hand.

Opening her lungs, she took a gasping breath as she broke the surface of deep consciousness. Only after removing her hands from Jason's chest did she remember she was the only thing holding him up. He slumped toward her. "Shoot. Sorry." Catching him by the shoulders, she lowered him to the floor, noticing the thick cords of muscle in his arms. He'd gained weight during their time together. He was bigger. Heavier.

"Jason?"

He blinked up at her as if waking from a deep sleep. "Did you get it? Do I have… light?"

"Yes." She laughed. "You have a strong anchor, a memory so perfect I didn't want to leave it."

He pushed himself up on his elbows.

"You should have something to eat and drink. Was it as bad as last time? Do you feel nauseous?"

Jason sat up the rest of the way and rubbed the back of his neck. "Not as bad. I'm groggy but I feel okay."

"Come on, I'll make you some tea." She held out her hand to him but he rose without her help. Selene thought he looked stronger as he moved past her to the kitchen where he began filling the teapot.

"So, what was this memory?" he asked. He placed the teapot on the stove and lit the burner.

"You were fifteen, sitting at the table with Laina and Silas. Your mother was making gingerbread cookies." Selene paused because Jason had gone ghost white. "What's wrong?"

"Nothing. I… I think… excuse me." He strode from the room without another word, leaving Selene staring confusedly into an empty kitchen.

SEVENTEEN

Jason flopped on his bed. Why had it been that memory? As soon as Selene had mentioned the cookies, the day had come back to him, a day he'd felt truly loved. It was one of the last days they were all together. Weeks later, Silas would move back to college and, although there would be visits, they would never live under the same roof again.

His stomach flipped as he remembered his parents dancing in the kitchen. It was something they'd done often, a quirky thing he'd found embarrassing as a teenager and oddly out of character for his usually stoic father. Now he'd do anything to see his parents dancing.

Outside his room, he heard Selene digging through his cupboards, pots and pans banging together, cabinet doors opening and closing. He should get up and help her find whatever she was looking for, but he didn't. He was too busy trying to forget the memory she'd recalled in him. What she didn't understand was that his happiest memory was now his most brutal reminder of his parents' murder.

How could he tell Selene that remembering the source of the light within him was what fueled the darkness? A spray of bullets stole that moment from him in the most brutal way possible, negating it and every happy moment that came before. It was a memory of how everything you loved turned to shit eventually. Worm fodder.

Suddenly exhausted, he threaded his fingers behind his head, closed his eyes, and forced himself to forget again as he drifted away.

* * * * *

Gingerbread. The scent was unmistakable and almost overwhelming to his hypersensitive wolf senses. Immediately, the memory came back to him, all its light and its resulting darkness filling him at once.

"Selene, what have you done?" He scowled. Bounding from the bed, he burst from his room, ready to give her a piece of his mind. But when he reached the kitchen, the sight of her thawed any ice that had formed around his heart.

She'd donned a dress, the first one he'd ever seen her wear, simple and conservative with a flowing skirt that reached below the knee. Her hair was down, loose curls draped over her shoulders and flowing to the center of her back. And her smile was bright enough to light up the room.

All he could think was that she was perfect, beautiful, and worthy like an angel dropped down from heaven. Selene pulled a tray of cookies from the oven and turned her violet eyes on him.

"Who's ready for some cookies?" she said softly.

Jason's throat constricted and a muscle in his jaw twitched. Eyes burning, he crossed to her, a confusing mix of emotions swirling in his head. He shook her by the shoulders.

"Oww. Jason, you're hurting me."

A growl emanated from his chest, his wolf lowering its head and baring its teeth. Her eyes widened.

This close with his hands wrapped around her upper arms, he was more than aware how his size dwarfed hers. He'd gained the weight back, thanks to her, and now he was using it against her.

Justifiably. She had yanked his chain one too many times.

"Why would you do this?" he said. "Why would you do this to me?"

"I… I thought you needed help remembering. I wanted to recreate the moment. Sometimes a smell can bring it back." She squirmed within his too-tight grip.

"I remember, Selene. I remember everything about that day," he said through his teeth. "But did it ever occur to you that that memory holds nothing but pain for me?"

Tears formed in her eyes. "You're hurting me," she whispered.

He shook her harder. "They're dead. Every time I think of how perfect our family was, I remember what Alex took from me. He's still out there somewhere, probably being nursed back to health by an evil dragon bitch, and everything that was right and good about my life is gone. Think about what this means. You are telling me that my core memory, the thing that brings light to my soul, is something I can never have again. How can you believe for a second that I can ever leave my vice behind when the darkness is the only thing holding me together? There's no hope for anything else. Everything that was good about me is dead."

Trembling, Selene twisted from Jason's grip. A tear slipped from the corner of her eye, carving a path down the slope of her nose to her upper lip. "Everything good about you is *not* dead," she said softly. "I wouldn't be here if I thought the light in you had died." She rubbed her shoulders, backing away. "Alex didn't take everything from you. There are still people who believe in you. People who need you."

"Like who?"

"Silas… and Laina."

Jason rolled his eyes.

"The pack. All the people whose businesses you invest in."

"Silas is more alpha than any pack needs, including ours. And you don't need light in your soul to make a good investment."

"Me." Selene's gaze lifted to his. "I need you." Her voice was as brittle as a dried bone.

He licked his lips. "Yeah. You need me to get better so you can be promoted to priestess." He snorted derisively.

"No. That's not it." Selene's voice was laden with emotion as if she were on the verge of tears.

"Then why?"

"Because… because…" She shook her head.

He began to turn, to walk away. Her hand landed on his. Selene guided one hand around her waist and his other into her upturned grip. Jason didn't fight her as she pulled him into her chest.

"Selene, what are you doing?"

Without answering, she began to sway. It took a moment for him to take the lead, for her movement to stop battling his stillness, but soon their bodies moved as one. He rocked back and forth, turning her as they crossed the floor, and never breaking eye contact. He tried not to think about the fact she was an acolyte and his spiritual advisor or that everything that was happening fell well within the bounds of "inappropriate." He was greedy and the tiny slice of happiness Selene was offering was not something he was willing to turn away.

He held her closer, his face a breath away from hers, and then, without warning, spun her away from his chest, across the kitchen, and back into his arms, dipping her in front of the stove. She giggled, her laugh ringing through him like a bell and lifting two tons of weight from his heart.

"You're stunning," he whispered in her ear as if it were a secret. "Do you know you could have any man you ever wanted with a wink of your eye?"

"Don't be silly," she said breathlessly. "I've never been beautiful."

"Oh, sweet girl, you're wrong about that, and if you were mine you'd never forget it."

She met his eyes, her lip tucking between her teeth in a gesture that made her look younger than she was. He stood her on her own two feet, realizing his wolf's interest in her had grown to unsafe levels for both of them. As much as he wanted her, as much as he longed to have her goodness in his life permanently, he needed to accept that she was here in a professional capacity only. She might remain friendly with him when all was said and done, but she'd never be his. Not really.

But then why wasn't she moving away from his open arms?

* * * * *

A chill came over Selene's body as Jason set her on her feet and opened his arms, the absence of his touch like the loss of heat after the setting sun. His green eyes darkened, a storm gathering in his thoughts, the irises tinged with amber. In that moment, she was not an acolyte or a spiritual therapist, she was just a woman whose entire being wanted to be back in those arms, wanted to feel *precious* again, wanted a taste of something she'd never had before, never would have again.

She stepped into his space and rose up on her tiptoes, her arms snaking around his neck. His breath quickened with his pulse, his hands spreading wider as if he were afraid to touch her, and his face, oh goddess, his face was a mask of torment. Ignoring the alarms going off in her head, she planted a kiss on his lips. She'd never kissed a man like this. Sure she'd had a mouth forced upon hers. She'd been kissed. But she'd never done the kissing. And certainly a kiss had never felt like this one. Soft, warm, gentle, searching. Her mind blanked, wrapped up in all the emotions and raw feelings that came with her wanton exploration.

But the kiss was one sided, his body stiff, his lips accepting but tentative. Until, quite suddenly, the wall she'd been pressing against, the invisible thing holding him back, shattered. His arms wrapped around her ribs and swept her away, the storm she'd seen gathering in his eyes swirling around her. The full force of his masculinity beat against her lips, blew across her skin, and doused her body in a deluge of heat. His hands were in her hair, on her waist.

And he was inside her mouth, stroking her tongue with his own in a way that set her on fire. His body pressed against hers, ushering her toward the sofa. When she bumped into its rounded back, he lifted her, hoisting her dress so he could slide between her knees.

Was this really happening? His body held a coiled tension she instinctively knew she could release. If she didn't know better, she'd say it was magic, this force driving them toward each other. She wrapped her arms tighter around his neck, drawing him closer until she could feel the hard length of him pressed against her.

Jason pulled back, panting and groaning as if he were in pain. "No. No, we can't."

Selene shook her head. "This is right. It's all right." Something in the back of her mind knew she was wrong, but she didn't want to think about it. Not now. Not yet. She wanted to stay in the storm, feel the rain drench her face, get swept away by the wind and the lightning without a thought to the consequences.

"You'd regret it. It would mean the end of your acolyte status. And as much as I want you, and oh, by the goddess I want you, I can't do that to you. I can't take your virtue when I know you'd never do this if I hadn't been such a shit to you and drawn you into my web."

"Drew me in? I wasn't drawn in. I have feelings for you—"

"You're sweet and naive. You don't see it. I'm a predator. I have a power over women. It's not your fault. Without even realizing it, I seduced you. You'd never do this if I hadn't. You'd never risk your future." He backed away, his hands coming to rest on his knees, the physical hardship of holding back the desires of his wolf evident on his face.

Selene's eyes widened and she looked out the glass doors to the balcony, to the moon that hung in the night sky. "I'm so sorry, Jason. I'm a fool."

"It's not you."

"No. The shift is tomorrow night. I've tempted you at your most vulnerable."

He took a step back, still hunched over, and clutched his middle.

"Are you in pain?"

"Go into your room and lock the door," he said.

"What? Jason, no. Let's talk about this."

He raised his eyes to hers and all she saw was the animal, the intense need turning his eyes from green to the amber of his wolf's. She hopped down from the back of the couch.

"Go," he said, a deep growl emanating from his chest.

She did, running into her room and locking the door. She heard him pacing on the other side for some time, the slam of what she assumed was the cookie sheet against the counter, the whine of the front door opening, and his groans as Silas's command kept him from leaving.

Eventually, after what seemed like hours of painful pacing, his bedroom door slammed and she heard his shower turn on.

Selene fell back onto her bed, wondering at the ache in her body that accompanied her thoughts of Jason. She ran her fingers down her neck, between her breasts, over the cotton bodice of her dress, and up along her inner thigh. She stopped at the lace edge of her briefs. Was a vice catching? Because right now, all Selene could think of, although she knew it was wrong and self-destructive, was how she didn't regret kissing Jason.

If anything, she regretted stopping.

EIGHTEEN

"You finished the cookies," Selene said, setting down the brown plaid suitcase she'd been holding. Sun streamed in through the east-facing windows, but it did nothing to warm her.

Jason gave her an exhausted smile before his eyes locked on her bag. "What's with the suitcase?"

"I think you proved last night that you don't need me anymore. You have full control over your vice. Tonight is the shift. If you can deny yourself so close to the full moon, there's nothing left for me to teach you."

"Oh, I'm not sure about that," he murmured.

She shook her head and looked at the floor.

"For one, I need someone to show me how to make the cookies you made last night. I've never baked anything like that. And someone to hold my hand when I feel sick like you did. Someone to remind me of happy memories. Someone to fill this place with joy and light like you have." He stood and approached her.

"I suspect you'll have no trouble finding a woman to do all those things. And when the time is right and Nickelova is dead, you can build a life with her."

"But she won't be you."

"She can't be me." Selene swallowed the lump that had formed in her throat. "No matter how badly I want that."

Jason took another step toward her, his hands spread as if approaching a skittish animal. "You want this too?" He searched her face. "Then why are you leaving?"

"You don't want me, Jason. It's natural for a man like you to attach to a caregiver. But once you're back out in the world, you'll realize I'm nothing special. I'm no one, just an orphan living among your pack. And my feelings for you, there's no way to separate them from what happened here."

"You're wrong—"

"My work here is done. If I stay now, I'd only be fostering a dependence we'd both have to break."

He shook his head. "No. That's not what this is. You know that's not what this is."

"I give you permission to leave. You're free. You've graduated from my care. I'll let Silas know and I'll see you at Rivergate for the shift tonight." She lifted her bag and headed for the door.

"Selene?"

She paused, turning back to him.

"Thank you. I'd be dead if it wasn't for you. I'll never forget that."

With a soft smile and a nod, she said, "In some ways, I could say the same." She slipped out the door and left Jason standing in his foyer.

* * * * *

Selene returned to the monastery feeling numb. She was doing the right thing. Of course she was. The feelings she'd felt for Jason were a natural extension of the therapy she'd administered. Therapists of all kinds were at risk of falling in love with their patients. She'd seen his darkest parts and his happiest memories. She'd shared things about herself she'd never shared with anyone. In time, she'd get on with her real life and those memories would shed like an old snakeskin to some recess of her mind.

When that happened, when she started to forget how happy she was with Jason, how even when he was sick or angry or nearly dead his smile had lit up her soul. When those memories dulled, the pain in her chest would stop, and she'd be thankful she was strong today. A person needed to be logical about these things. Love and sex and loneliness were tricky, all mashed up with one another. Time and distance would sort it out.

She rocked backward to fling her suitcase onto the bed, her long skirt catching on the corner. She smoothed the material down, then unzipped her bag to start unpacking. She'd had the plaid brown monstrosity since she was a kid. It had served her well. But maybe this time, it would stay unpacked.

"Welcome back," Artemis said from behind her. "I thought I saw you coming through the gate."

Selene smiled. "It's good to be home again." She accepted Artemis's embrace.

"I assume your return is a positive sign. Was your mission effective?"

"Jason has complete control over his vice. I am confident he has been successfully rehabilitated."

"Hmm." Artemis nodded. "I knew you were the right choice for this assignment. Congratulations. A novice acolyte could not have performed the deep spiritual cleansing you did."

Eyes focused on the folded clothes within her suitcase, Selene hummed affirmatively.

"Why do I sense unhappiness within you?"

"Artemis, I have to tell you something. I… made a mistake last night. Or maybe you might call it an accident. There was an accident."

The older woman steadied Selene's trembling hands with her own.

"What happened, child? This is a safe place. You can tell me anything."

"We kissed. Jason and I kissed. I kissed him." The words bubbled out of her, extricating themselves and flooding her with relief.

Artemis's eyes widened, although her face remained impassive. "Go on."

"I was trying to jog his happiest memory. I got too close. We were dancing, and I kissed him. He stopped the kiss, thank the goddess. But it happened."

"How did you feel about the kiss?"

Selene's cheeks warmed. She wasn't expecting Artemis to ask her that question. She placed a cool hand to her cheek. "It was pleasant and shocking. Afterward, I knew it was wrong but when it was happening it felt like jumping over a waterfall. Exhilarating. Weightless. Almost as if I couldn't stop it if I tried."

"With an inevitable crash waiting for you at the bottom." Artemis laughed.

"Can you forgive me?" Selene pressed a hand to her chest.

Artemis started. "Forgive you? Whatever for?"

"Men are off-limits to our order."

She tipped her curly gray head. "The encounter ended after the kiss?"

"Yes. But in full disclosure, it was quite passionate."

"Do you know why we remain celibate here?"

"In honor of the goddess. Our virtue is an offering to her and in exchange, she gives us power."

Artemis nodded. "Your encounter went too far. You kissed. But you are here and your virtue is intact." She spread her hands. "It is understandable that the experience was confusing to you, but the fact that you told me about it immediately speaks boldly of your character. I am not concerned at all about this incident. You are a very talented spiritual leader, Selene. Add this experience to the many things to come that will help you grow in your faith and abilities."

Selene nodded. "Oh, thank you, *Preotka*." She turned back to her bag feeling light as air. "I should unpack."

"Unless…" Artemis folded her long, graceful arms over her cardigan and narrowed her eyes on Selene.

Selene blinked at her mentor.

"Love is a rare and powerful gift from the goddess. If you genuinely have feelings for Jason, and he returns those feelings, perhaps it is a sign from above that there is a more important role for you in this life than priestess."

Selene gave a breathy laugh. "What could be more important than priestess?"

Artemis didn't miss a beat. "Devoted wife, loving mother, conscientious princess, practitioner of true love. My dear Selene, if you have been blessed with love, do not allow it to slip through your fingers."

"But how would I know? I know nothing of love." Selene bit her lip. "Artemis, have you ever… been in love?"

Artemis shook her head. "Only with the pack."

Selene dropped her arms to her sides in frustration and stared at her feet. "This is silly. It was only a kiss. Nothing more."

With a knowing smile, Artemis nodded. "I thought so. But if you do decide it's something more, remember this isn't a prison. You can leave if you want to."

Selene lifted a stack of clothes from her bag and laid them out on the bed. "But there's no coming back," she said.

Artemis cleared her throat. "No. There's no coming back."

NINETEEN

Jason's thoughts refused to stay in the present as he wandered through the garden at Rivergate Manor under a canopy of silvery sunset and slowly emerging stars. He'd tried to stop thinking about Selene and to focus on his business, which was sorely in need of his attention. But he'd failed miserably. His scout, Andrew, informed him that the Spackles deal was officially dead because of his neglect. But as much as he would have liked to return to business as usual, his mind bounced right back to Selene.

It wasn't just his wolf's innate desire to mark her as his own, although that part was surely there. His heart ached for her. He'd spent the day pacing an empty apartment, remembering how full it felt with her in it. Like a real home.

"Welcome back, brother." Silas broke into Jason's thoughts with a pat on his shoulder as he sidled up next to him. "Selene gave me a glowing review of your willpower and constraint this morning."

Jason adjusted his watch on his wrist, remembering how little restraint he'd shown when he was shoving his tongue down her throat the night before. "It's good to be back," he said mechanically.

"You've certainly put on some weight. Jesus, you're going to pop a button with all the muscle going on under there."

"Funny how a few weeks locked in one's home revives their love of physical activity." Based on his brother's expression, the note of bitterness in his words wasn't lost on Silas.

"It was necessary. I know it wasn't easy, but now you're ready to face Nickelova if she comes for you. That's what's important."

"So, when can we try to find her and kill her?"

"After the shift. I've rounded up three wolves, all with military experience. Gerty has agreed to go too. Grateful can't leave her son but has promised to provide magical protection in the form of potions and spells. Do you think you can remember where to go?"

He nodded. "I remember." Jason couldn't wait to destroy the dragon fae who had started all this, made him suffer, only to find true happiness with Selene and experience true suffering all over again when she left. He wanted the dragon bitch to die slowly, but he'd take her death however he could get it. He hoped he was the one to do it, preferably by crushing her heart between his own two hands.

They arrived at the tent where the pack was shedding clothes in preparation for the shift.

"See you on the other side of the moon." Silas crossed to the opposite side of the tent to strip.

Jason removed his tailored shirt and pants, toed off his leather loafers, and folded everything in a neat pile in the corner. He left the tent completely naked, his blood bubbling under the surface of his skin. The change was close at hand.

That's when he saw her. Selene locked eyes with him across the sparsely wooded lawn, her beautiful skin gleaming in the moonlight. From the moment he'd met her, he'd admired the way she carried herself, like she lived above the fray, and now was no exception. Her hair was down. Goddess, he loved her hair. The delicate bones of her face added to the long stretch of her body, giving her the look of a ballerina, graceful even in the face of impending pain, an angel in their midst.

The din of the older members of the pack starting to shift filled the space: groans and growls and breaking bones. Jason pitched forward, the tawny fur of his underside breaking out along his abdomen. Human thought was difficult in this state as his wolf mind started taking over, but the last clear thought he had before he changed was a raging need to claim Selene as his. *Mine,* his wolf whispered. *Mine.*

And then he surrendered completely to the animal within.

* * * * *

The next morning, light poured over Selene's body, the scent of new grass filling her lungs. Spring signified new life. Tiny hatching eggs deep within fresh earth. Budding green things. Blooming moss. Fresh dew. But it was another smell that made her spine stiffen. The warm spicy scent of male, musky cloves and chicory, a male whose arm draped across her stomach.

She might have turned in her half slumber to confirm who it was, but with a sleepy grunt the owner of the arm pulled her against a wide muscled chest. Glancing down at the hand between her naked breasts, she didn't need to see his face. Dark hair dappled thick cords of muscle in the forearm. Strong hands held her. She knew this man. Knew his scent. It was Jason.

A werewolf was not responsible for what he or she did in wolf form. It was commonly accepted that a person's wolf had a mind of its own. But lying here in Jason's arms, every second brought her deeper into the realization that it wasn't just her wolf who'd enjoyed Jason's company. She could hardly bring herself to move from the pleasure of his closeness.

Moving only her eyes, she glanced around them. They were inside a closely set group of trees, and they were alone. She pretended to be asleep and snuggled in closer, closing her eyes as the feel of his breath on her hair sent tiny sparks of longing down the length of her neck and across the surface of her skin.

His hand coasted over her nipple, along the flat length of her torso and rounded the curve of her hip. Goddess, it was delectable. A warm ache ignited in her core, her need opening like a flower. She crossed her legs against the feeling, suppressing the moan his touch elicited.

She felt the moment he woke, the realization of her closeness causing his body to tense. He removed his hand from her hip and whispered, "Sorry" into the back of her head. As he rolled away from her, she knew she should act as though she were sorry too, cover up, move away. But she didn't.

Instead, she rolled onto her back and looked up at him, naked, vulnerable. He was balanced on his elbow beside her, hovering but not touching. When their gazes met, her longing was so intense, her body began to tremble. Tears streamed down her face.

"Oh goddess, I'm so sorry. Did my wolf hurt you? Should I get help?" Jason whispered.

Selene shook her head. She wiped under her eyes. "It's not you or your wolf," she said softly. "It's me. Lying here next to you, I can't pretend…"

He frowned, his eyes narrowing. "Can't pretend what?"

"I can't pretend that I'm not jealous of my wolf." She sobbed quietly. "I wish things were different. I wish I had the freedom to feel what I feel."

He swallowed audibly, cleared his throat. "What do you feel?"

"I'm falling in love with you, Jason," she said, the words tumbling out all at once. "For the first time, I'm questioning what I want for my future. This isn't supposed to happen. I'm supposed to keep a professional distance. But every time I close my eyes, I see you." She turned her head to look away from him. "I'm a terrible person. I've betrayed my role as an acolyte."

A shadow passed over her face, his hand hovering, almost as if he were afraid to touch her. She thought he might pull it away, but then he wiped her tears with his thumb. He stroked along her jaw, encouraging her to face him.

"You are not a terrible person," he said quietly. "Why does this have to be a mistake? Can't you see that I've fallen for you, too? I don't care if it's because of the therapy or if we were just meant to be together. By the goddess, you've gotten under my skin. If you feel the same way, don't we owe it to ourselves to see where this goes?"

Selene blinked up at him and scoffed. "You don't understand. I can't just try you on for size. If I pursue this, there's no going back for me. I'd have to give up my status as an acolyte."

Jason's brow furrowed. "I'm not suggesting you *try me on for size*. I'm talking about something exclusive and permanent. I've never had that before. I know it won't be easy, but I want to try with you."

He removed his hand from her face and shifted as though he might get up and walk away.

Goddess help her, she couldn't deny this anymore. Selene reached out and caught him behind the neck. At first he looked surprised. He gripped her wrist, searching her face.

"Try," she whispered. "I want to try."

A muscle in his jaw twitched. "I've learned to restrain myself around you, Selene, but make no mistake, I've wanted you, my wolf has wanted you, since the moment I saw you standing under that tree in Red Grove. You don't know what you do to me. You're playing with fire." His eyes flared amber. His presence loomed like a growing hunger above her. "Do you know what you want? Because I do, and I don't think I can resist you anymore."

In answer, she pulled his face toward hers. A rumble came from deep inside his chest and his mouth slanted across hers, the kiss warm and soft, a question instead of a demand. Her arms snaked around his neck, gripping him tighter. He licked the crease of her lips, an invitation she was more than happy to accept. The erotic feel of his tongue stroking against hers made a rush of heat flare inside her. With a sharp inhale, his body responded to her arousal, covering her, surrounding her. His elbows landed on either side of her head as his fingers buried in her hair.

Her hand stroked along his side, skimming over his warm skin, then up and over the peaks and hollows of his back. She used her nails to pull him closer, scoring his skin. He groaned into her mouth.

Breaking away, Jason panted, his chest heaving. "This isn't the right time or place. Not here. Not now." She was surprised that it was Jason who said it. Wasn't she supposed to be the one to protest? "I want it to be special for you. Our first time should be memorable."

Only, she didn't want to wait. She didn't want the opportunity to think or to change her mind. "Please," she said against his lips. She guided his hand down her inner thigh and between her legs.

Amber eyes flashed, a growl vibrating against her chest. His fingers stroked her, circling her opening with a tantalizing rhythm. By the time he dipped inside, she was quivering. Her body rolled beneath his touch, his expert hands coaxing a rush of pleasure from her core. She arched, creating counterpressure against his hand.

His thumb circled and his fingers thrust before he dipped his head. She felt his lips below her belly button, his tongue tracing circles toward his fingers. It was too much. Her face blazed thinking of him *down there*. But if her mind wished to protest, the rest of her suppressed that urge as Jason's tongue licked up her center.

She spread her arms on the soft moss and arched into him. Two more languid licks and she shattered, her body clenching around his fingers, tiny sparks of pleasure blowing out through her fingertips before echoing back to her core.

He held her as the aftershocks rocked her body. Stroking her hair back, his hips settling between her legs. He hesitated to enter her.

"Let's make this real. I don't want shadows or secrecy with you." His eyes pleaded with her. "I want the world to know you're mine."

"I'll have to step down from my position."

He searched her face, his jaw tightening. A deep breath moved in and out of his lungs. He suddenly looked gravely serious. "I can't ask you to do that."

"You don't have to. I want to. It's the right thing to do. It's time to make a choice, and I…" She ran her fingers across his chest. "Well, I already have. I choose you."

A smile spread across his face—until Silas's burly hand clamped down on the back of his neck and lifted him off her in one swift movement.

"What have you done?"

TWENTY

Jason's back slammed against the nearest tree, Silas holding him there with a stiff forearm to his neck.

"No. Stop!" Selene cried.

Silas ignored her. "You fucking asshole. Taking advantage of an acolyte! I should beat you senseless for this."

Jason tried to speak but his windpipe failed under Silas's crushing weight.

Selene shoved against Silas's massive chest as she wedged her waifish body between the two men. "Stop! It wasn't Jason. He didn't do anything wrong."

Silas looked at her in confusion.

"It was me! I'm in love with your brother."

Jason shoved Silas away from Selene, his newly increased size translating into a more powerful thrust than he'd intended. Silas stumbled backward, growling and baring his teeth.

"This isn't what you think," Jason said. "Just forget you saw anything. It will work itself out soon enough."

Selene held up her hands, a look of panic on her face. Jason longed to wipe the tears from her eyes, hated that his feelings for her were ripping her apart. He wished he could make it easier for her, but no one could turn back time. He couldn't unlove her and he wouldn't turn her away if she loved him back.

"Please. Please don't tell anyone. I'm not ready," she said to Silas. "I will tell Artemis. Give me a chance to tell her myself."

With a shake of his head, Silas seemed to contemplate her words, pacing and cursing to himself. "This… this isn't going to go over well with the pack. How could this happen?"

"Please, Silas." Selene folded her arms over her stomach.

After more grumbling, Silas placed his hands on his hips and let out a deep breath. "You two can't walk back together. People will talk. You"—he pointed at Jason—"go back the long way. Selene, wait five minutes and take the direct route. I don't know what's going on here, but I'll give you the next two days to get your heads on straight. After that, I'll expect action and answers."

Jason glanced at Selene who seemed amicable to the arrangement. "Fair," he said.

When he reached out for her to say good-bye, Silas thrust a hand between them and shook his head. "I'm not the only one out here."

With one last look at Selene, Jason obeyed his brother and jogged toward Rivergate Manor.

* * * * *

Alone among the trees, Selene waited, hugging herself against the cool spring air. She'd have to tell Artemis, move out of the monastery, try to find a job and a temporary place to live. She was fairly confident that Jason would help her. He was wealthy after all. She wouldn't ask him for money, but he might have connections. Perhaps there was a werewolf family in need of a nanny. She'd always been good with children.

As she paced, a high-pitched keening met her ears, the bleat of a dying animal. She wandered toward the sound, peering through a thick web of tree branches. A deer. Mauled by a wolf, by the looks of it. She frowned. It was odd for her kind to kill what it did not eat. Unless… it might have been her or Jason who'd done it, perhaps becoming distracted with each other and not finishing their meal. Well, she couldn't just leave it to suffer. She pushed through the thick line of trees and strode toward the doe, intending to break its neck. But when she reached it, the strangest thing happened. The doe changed. She'd seen it move, watched its throat constrict with its screams. But now it was dead. For some time, by the looks of it. An old, rotting kill. She shook her head. Was she hallucinating from the stress?

"He doesn't mean it," came a woman's voice from behind her.

Selene whirled to face a svelte woman with a platinum blond bob. Her skin was smooth as marble and her features as sharp as if they were chiseled from the same. She was wearing a red wrap dress that showed off a curvy figure. But it was the talisman around her neck that gave her away: a twisting dragon with a red stone eye. It looked to be made of pewter but she knew better. It was dragon scale.

"Nickelova." Selene eyed the line of trees behind the woman in horror. She'd been so caught up thinking about Jason, she unwittingly crossed the border, moved beyond the protective enchantment of Rivergate Manor. She hugged herself harder, suddenly feeling more naked than a moment before.

"He's a dog," Nickelova said. "He uses women and throws them away. He used me. Then, when I asked him for help, he dropped me like a hot stone."

"Jason didn't drop you. You tried to kill him and his siblings," Selene said, hoping her words were enough of a distraction that she could make it to the safety of Rivergate. She inched in that direction.

"Did he tell you that? It's refreshing to know he speaks of me at all. But it appears I am at a disadvantage. I didn't know about you until today." She frowned. "My curse should have brought Jason to my door by now. When the full moon rose again and he still didn't come to me, I realized there was a problem. No way could he go this long without sex. Not Jason. Imagine my surprise to track him here only to see him, to feel him"—she ran a finger along her bottom lip—"with you. Such a tender moment. That sort of thing should have triggered my curse. It seems someone has interfered with my magic. You wouldn't know anything about that, would you?" Her eyebrows knit.

Selene said nothing.

"Did you think I wouldn't suspect anything? Did he think I wouldn't check on him when he didn't follow my instructions?" Her face contorted, rage turning her elegant features ugly.

Selene darted for the border, running as fast as she could in a wide arc around Nickelova. But one pulse of the dragon fae amulet and her muscles locked in place as rigid as if she'd been turned to stone from the neck down. She cursed.

"What's your name, wolf?"

"Go to hell," Selene said.

The dragon amulet flashed again and Selene's throat constricted. The force at her neck lifted her onto her tiptoes. "Say your name."

"Se… lene…" she rasped, clawing at her throat. The tightening eased and she dropped to her feet again, pitching forward to take deep gasping breaths.

"Selene, I think once you get to know me, we are going to be great friends."

"I don't plan to get to know you," Selene said between pants.

"You don't have a choice. I want Jason's help, and I have a feeling that all he needs to see things my way is a little motivation. Judging by what just went on between you two, I think you are exactly what I'm looking for."

Selene screamed as her body lurched with another pulse of Nickelova's amulet. All the air was sucked from her lungs as a rush of darkness overtook her. A moment later, she landed somewhere hard and cold and totally alone.

* * * * *

Jason had just fastened the last button on his dress shirt when he heard Selene's scream. He ignored the questioning murmurs around him and broke into a dead run, taking the short way back to the place where they'd been, the direction of the scream. But when he reached the tightly grouped trees, she was gone.

"Selene! Selene!"

"She went this way," Silas said, arriving behind him and sniffing the air. The two brothers walked to the tree-lined border of the property and stopped. "She passed beyond the protective boundary."

"Why? Why would she do that?"

"There's a kill." Silas pointed at a dead doe. He approached the carcass, carefully picking his way through the tight web of branches that signified the border. "Do you smell that?"

Jason caught a whiff of someone other than Selene, a dangerous scent he hadn't smelled in weeks. "Dragon magic." A hard lump formed in his throat.

"Fuck." Silas dug his fingers into his wild hair.

Jason's phone rang. He slid it from his pocket, glancing at Silas when he saw who was calling. He tapped the screen and raised it to his ear.

"Jason?" said the familiar, dark voice, edged in gravel. "Ryker from Lost Things."

"This isn't a good time."

"Something just arrived in my store for you."

"What? What are you talking about? Arrived? Did someone bring something in?"

"No, Mr. Flynn. This item appeared where before there was nothing. I think you'd better take a look. I'm sending a picture now."

Jason heard the chirp of a text coming in. One look and he doubled over. "No. No. No."

"It smells of dragon," Ryker said.

"What is it?" Silas asked. "Show me."

Jason held up his phone, his hand trembling so hard he was surprised his brother could make out the picture. But the item was unmistakable. A ponytail of caramel-colored hair lay across the counter at Lost Things, labeled with a simple note. *For Jason Flynn.*

TWENTY-ONE

"Nickelova took Selene." Jason couldn't breathe. This was a living nightmare, the worst possible scenario. He knew Nickie would come back for *him*. It never once occurred to him that she might target Selene.

Silas grabbed the phone out of Jason's hand. "Who is this guy Ryker? How do we know he's not helping Nickelova?"

"He's a business associate." Jason's voice trembled with a mixture of anger and fear. "Look, Nickie wants me to follow her clues. She's always wanted that. She won't free Selene unless I go to her." Jason strode toward Rivergate.

"You'll be walking right into her trap!" Grabbing his elbow, Silas whirled him around. "She's expecting you to do something rash. She's using Selene as bait."

Jason bit his lip. "And I can't keep her dangling from the hook."

"You'll have to shift again tonight. You'll be vulnerable," Silas said.

"I'll also be at my strongest."

"Until you're not you anymore. The wolf is unpredictable. You could get Selene killed."

"I'll take my chances."

"Wait until after the shift, Jason," Silas said. "Nickelova won't hurt Selene because she needs the hold over you. It'll give us time to prepare."

"I am not going to leave Selene in the clutches of that madwoman a moment longer than I have to."

"You can't do this alone."

"I can't wait for the others." Jason shook his head and pulled his elbow from Silas's grip.

"Just… give me until tonight." Silas strode quickly, side by side with Jason. "Let me talk to Gerty and Grateful. I'll put together a team."

Jason ground his teeth.

"Promise me you'll wait. Just until tonight. Until we have a plan." Silas was asking for his trust. His brother had earned that much. And his logic was sound.

Jason nodded. "What other choice do I have?"

Silas paused and pulled Jason into a hug. "We're going to get her back, brother."

"Right." Jason parted ways with Silas, heading for the parking lot while his brother took off toward Rivergate Manor. Thank the goddess his brother hadn't given him a direct alpha command. He hated to lie, but when it came to Selene, Jason was singularly focused. "Sorry, brother, but I made this mess—now I intend to clean it up."

* * * * *

"Do you have anything in this hoarder's dream of a shop that can kill a dragon fae?" Jason asked Ryker. Selene's ponytail was draped across his hands, her soft hair a gauntlet thrown at his feet. At least there was no blood. Nickelova could have left her entire head. No, this invitation was also a promise, although one he assumed had a time limit.

"Many things in my shop could be used as tools capable of killing a dragon fae, but wielding them is another matter entirely. All work in the same way. A dragon is immortal until you cut out its heart."

"A sword or a dagger, then?" Jason perused the stacks of dusty artifacts around him. "Which one won't curse me like the ring you sold me?"

Ryker's dark eyes flashed. "I warned you about the ring. You wouldn't listen."

Jason nodded. "Yes, yes, you warned me. Excuse me for being moody. A dragon has my girlfriend, Ryker. I need help and I need it fast."

"I thought I recognized this as Selene's," Ryker said, stroking the hair. Jason yanked the ponytail away from his fingers. "Pity. I liked the girl. She had pluck."

"So, find something to help me rescue her."

Ryker's tattoo glowed and his eyes flashed with red fire. He scanned the stacks of seemingly unorganized artifacts. Blowing like a dark wind through the narrow aisles, he stopped at a shelf and selected a short silver rod. "Try this."

Careful not to touch anything, Jason navigated the stacks and caught up to Ryker. "What is it?" He gingerly lifted the cylinder between his thumb and forefinger like it might explode in his hand at any moment. The metal baton was about four inches long with a one-inch diameter. Aside from possibly being used to bludgeon Nickelova, he couldn't think why the item would be useful at all.

"Well? Give it some intent," Ryker said. "And your full grip." He tucked the cylinder into Jason's palm and squeezed.

Reflexively, Jason raised the hand holding the silver cylinder, withdrawing from Ryker's tight grip. Jagged blades emerged from each end, thin and razor sharp, with a metal-on-metal clang that resounded through the store. Jason laughed and loosened his grip. The blades retracted into the weapon.

"That's better," Ryker said. "This is the bladed staff of Ocebel, the ancient siren goddess. It will react to your intent and increase the speed and accuracy of your strikes when near water. Water magic is a counterbalance to fire magic. You'll find this helpful in more ways than one. I recommend bringing some of the wet stuff with you."

"So I cut out her heart and that will kill her?"

Ryker laughed. "No. Removing her heart will make her mortal and give you power over her." He floated between the stacks, his body going misty at the edges. "Once you have her heart, you can kill the fae if you so choose or manipulate her to do your will. The heart itself has magical properties, even if the fae is deceased, but keeping her alive and holding her heart will make her your slave."

"So I remove her heart." Jason rolled the cylinder in his palm. "And then I can kill her. Sounds easy enough."

Ryker laughed. "You do know that dragon fae can shift into actual dragons at will, don't you? Although, she'll avoid the shift if she can. If she shifts, she gives up human logic and consciousness."

"Just like a werewolf," Jason muttered.

"Exactly. If she shifts, she must rely on her dragon instincts. Not ideal in all situations. But make no mistake, those instincts will protect her heart with three tons of scaled muscle, razor-sharp teeth, and a barbed tail."

"Why can't anything be easy?" Jason activated the bladed staff again, testing its weight in his hand.

Ryker stroked his hairless chin and stared at him for a moment. "No offense, but playing the hero isn't exactly your modus operandi. This girl must be special."

Jason locked eyes with the demon. "She is. Saved-my-life, keep-her-forever special."

"I was surprised how eagerly she risked her life to find you the night she came to me."

"Thanks for looking out for her."

"It wasn't easy." He licked his lips. "Selene is a temptation for the senses."

Jason growled, turning one of the blades of the cylinder toward the demon.

"Relax, my friend. I know better than to bite the hand that feeds me."

Jason released his grip and the silver rod returned to its original state. "I assume I can borrow this on credit and return it when I'm finished. Or do you want payment upfront?"

"You can borrow it, for free, on one condition." Ryker's eyes filled with ruby fire. "As I mentioned, a dragon fae's heart has magical properties that a demon in my line of business would find exceptionally useful. Bring me the heart, and we'll call it even."

One of the skills Jason possessed that made him an excellent investor was his ability to read people. Ryker was a demon, but his intentions weren't evil. Self-serving, perhaps, but the guy had a moral code. His word was good, and most of the time, he spoke the truth.

"It's a deal," Jason said.

The demon tipped his head in affirmation. "Good luck, Jason Flynn. I certainly hope to see you, Selene, and the dragon's heart in my shop very soon."

Jason nodded and made his way out of the crowded store. There was much to do and this was only his first stop.

* * * * *

When Jason arrived at the Route 9 Bridge over Eagle River, he wasn't sure what he expected. Not a blinking neon sign that said *dragon this way,* but something, some clue that he was headed in the right direction. The picture Nickelova had implanted in his brain showed two mountains in the distance, beyond the forest he was looking at now. Only, standing here, with the road, the river, and everything else as pictured, the mountains were conspicuously absent. He took this as a sign. He would hike toward where the mountains should have been and trust that the way would reveal itself when he got close enough.

He tied the laces of his new hiking boots and donned the backpack of camping supplies he'd packed, checking that the silver cylinder was strapped to the side and well within reach. Then he sent Silas three texts. The first was a picture of his Bugatti in front of the Route 9 sign he'd told him about. The second was a picture of the place where the mountains should be. The third contained two simple words: "I'm sorry."

His phone rang almost immediately after he hit send, but he didn't answer. He couldn't risk Silas giving him a direct alpha command to return to

Rivergate. He needed to do this, and if he didn't go now, he might lose his nerve.

His brother was right. He was probably walking into a trap. That was semiobvious. But without a doubt, Jason couldn't live with himself another minute knowing she was there and he was here. He'd happily go to his death or to his slavery to save Selene. Silas would never let him do that, though. His brother didn't realize life meant nothing to Jason without her. He had to do this.

He turned off the phone and tossed it into his backpack. And then there was nothing but his boots and a narrow footpath that seemed to lead in the direction Nickelova wanted him to go.

* * * * *

Selene shivered in the darkness, her hands groping the stone floor beneath her. What had Nickelova done to her? One minute they were standing just outside the bounds of Rivergate and then she was here. It all seemed to happen in the blink of an eye. Only Selene had the oddest notion that she'd been unconscious for some time. The cold breeze on her neck seemed to confirm that hypothesis. Her hair was missing, cut short at her nape. When had that happened?

"Hello?" she called through a dry throat.

A fire blazed to life in an alcove of stone nearby, flooding the room with light. As her eyes adjusted, she took in the vast cavern around her. She was not alone.

"Welcome back from la-la land." Nickelova's high-heeled black boots click-clacked against the stone floor as she approached Selene. Stalagmites and stalactites broke the otherwise normal continuity of the room, which included a red Persian carpet and a plush-looking sofa near the fireplace.

Nickelova's posh appearance intimidated Selene. Her sleek platinum bob and tall, lanky build were something she associated with runway models, as was the red dress that wrapped around her body in a way that revealed more cleavage and leg than appropriate in mixed company. But it was the dragon-scale amulet around her neck that unsettled Selene the most. It throbbed with power as she neared.

"Jason won't come for me," Selene said. "I'm just an acolyte priestess who acted as his spiritual advisor. My life is not worth risking a member of the royal family."

"Hmm. Why do women like you constantly underestimate yourselves? You barely brush your hair, throw on any old rag that will cover you, and then creep around like a little mouse trying your best to be invisible. But clearly you are not invisible, Selene. The affection I witnessed Jason showing you was unusual for the man. For any man, actually. So, little mouse, it seems you've been noticed despite your best efforts."

Cheeks warming, Selene lowered her eyes. "I think you read more into it than there was."

Nickelova rolled her eyes. "Let me enlighten you. The curse I placed on Jason's vice was meant to force him to come to me. Obviously someone broke that curse. But part of my magic remains. A spell I placed on him long ago, on the evening we first met. You might call it a tracking device. It's how I found him and possessed that woman he was with in the first place. When he gets busy, I feel what he feels… I see what he sees. But oddly, I hadn't felt the tug of my curse in weeks. When I felt his *interaction* with you this morning, I went to him immediately, well, as close as I could get to the protective enchantment. I didn't just happen upon your rendezvous, Selene. In a way, I was watching you from the inside out. News flash: Jason loves you, little mouse." She said the last part through her teeth. "Let's stop pretending he doesn't. It wastes both our time."

Selene sputtered unintelligibly, trying her best to find the right words of denial, but Nickelova continued.

"I can't say I'm not jealous. I had hoped that *I* could be the one to master Jason's heart. But accommodations must be made. You will have to be the carrot on the stick. It's why I've kept you alive." Nickelova smiled wickedly, her eyes shifting to focus on something behind Selene.

Selene turned tentatively, only to let out a piercing scream. She was standing in front of a pile of bones. Human, animal, all mixed together in a grisly pile of death. Some were bleached, some burned, and some still clung to the remains of the flesh that once resided around them.

Hand clasped over her mouth and nose, she backed toward Nickelova, only to bump into a wall where there was no wall. After a frantic inspection of the area, she accepted the truth. She was a prisoner, jailed with a pile of bones behind an invisible barrier.

"No need for hysterics," Nickelova said. "A girl's gotta eat."

Selene turned from the bones and swallowed the bile rising in her throat. She was still naked but at least the fire Nickelova had started warmed the cave to a temperature that stalled her shivering.

"Why Jason? I thought you were helping Alex overthrow the Fireborn clan. Shouldn't you be after Silas? He's the alpha."

"Woman to woman?" Nickelova paced toward her, all fire and shadows. "Alex turned out to be a disappointment. See for yourself." She turned her body and pointed at the far wall of the cavern. Alex Ravien Bloodright was suspended like a specimen in a jar, embedded in the rocky wall. His eyes were closed, his hair and limbs floating in the reddish fluid. "He's healing," Nickelova said, "but slowly. He would have died weeks ago if not for my near-constant presence and the fire lily juice I stole from the fae hospital."

In her studies as an acolyte, Selene had read that dragons were once hunted almost to extinction for the power of their hearts. There was a reason Nickelova had stayed close to Alex in this cave, why she'd relied on her curse on Jason for information instead of the direct approach. The proximity of her heart was healing Alex, perhaps keeping him alive. Dragon heart could be used in the most dangerous of spells, even to raise the dead, according to certain holy texts. Nickelova was keeping Alex alive, but at what cost? If Alex was conscious at all, his state of being was horrific.

"Alex is too weak to do much more than sleep just now. When I wake him, he'll need someone strong to help us achieve our goals. We'll never take down Silas and rule the Lycanthropic Society without help."

"You don't want to kill Jason—you want him to join you." Selene shook her head. "You can't truly believe that will ever happen. He will never help you overthrow the council. He'd die before he'd betray the pack."

Turning toward the fire, Nickelova hugged herself, rubbing her outer arms. "He will… now that I have you. He's already on his way. I'll have him tamed in the amount of time it takes me to show him his dear, sweet Selene, dirty and shivering in my prison."

"You're wrong."

"The wolf in him won't be able to stand it, little mouse. The more enthusiastically he bows to me, the better your living conditions will get."

"No." Selene tucked her chin, her eyes burning. Why had she been so stupid? If she'd stayed away from Jason and maintained her vows as she should have, none of this would have ever happened.

"Don't fret. You both have the opportunity to be on the right side of history. When Alex and I rule the supernatural world, you'll be free to finally be your true self. For too long we've been forced into an existence based on balance and harmony."

"That is the law of the goddess," Selene said. "We must maintain balance or the world will fall into darkness and chaos."

"Some of us could do with a little darkness," she snapped. "Do you know that dragon fae are not a creation of the goddess?"

Selene furrowed her brow. Saying Nickelova was crazy was an understatement. "The goddess, Hecate, created all supernatural beings."

Nickelova scoffed. "No. Dragons, demons, and vampires were birthed from the underworld, created by the horned god, Panaal. Hecate and Panaal collaborated to design the reality we currently live in, rules and regulations based on a balance between the masculine and feminine. But Hecate is a wicked goddess. There is no balance. Dragons are almost extinct and demons and vampires live in the shadows. But when a dragon and a wolf rule the supernatural world, we'll change everything."

Selene shuddered to think how the world might change under the rule of Nickelova and Alex. Humans would likely be hunted to extinction. Or farmed by vampires. Werewolf children, human until their first shift, might become vampire targets, setting the two species at odds. Witches would likely be hunted by dragons who feared them due to their use of dragon parts in their spells. The most powerful witches, the demigoddesses known as Hecates, would be overwhelmed with their charge of maintaining balance and the management of their Hellmouth prisons. What Nickelova wanted would completely change life as they knew it. She had to be stopped. "You're mad. If what you're saying is true, you'd unleash the underworld."

Nickelova sighed. "That, little mouse, is the idea. Now, you'd better get some rest. Jason is on his way. You want to be strong enough to watch me break him, don't you?"

TWENTY-TWO

As the sun began to sink over the dense woods, Jason calculated he'd traveled about fifteen miles in the direction of the nonexistent mountains. He hadn't found a portal or any directions from Nickelova on how to reach her. Still, he was confident the dragon fae knew he was coming. Her spidey sense was powerful enough to detect when a fly entered her web.

Jason was no fool. He didn't labor under the delusion that he could sneak up on Nickelova's lair. On the contrary, he assumed he'd be invited in. That was the point, wasn't it? Once inside, he'd lie, cheat, beg, or steal to get Selene out alive. Then Nickelova could do with him what she would.

When he came upon a stream, he made camp, thankful for the fresh water and a safe, stony bank to start a fire. He pulled the chains and locks from his backpack. He wouldn't need a tent. In less than an hour he'd shift into wolf form and grow his own fur coat. All he had to do was keep the wolf contained until morning.

As the fire blazed to life, and he put a kettle of water on to prepare his freeze-dried meal, he undressed and crisscrossed the chains around his neck and chest. When he was confident the wolf would not be able to free itself, he padlocked himself to the nearest tree. No need to hide the key. Paws weren't good at using one.

He huddled inside his bedroll and ate four human helpings of the food he brought. As the sun dipped below the horizon and a full round moon came into view, he wondered what Nickelova was doing to Selene. Was she cold? In a place she could safely shift? Had she been fed? Clothed? The thought of her being tortured because of him made his stomach turn.

"Don't you hurt her," he yelled toward the place where the mountains should be. "Don't you hurt her, Nickelova!"

When his skin began to tingle and his bones to stretch, he used his last human strength to douse the flames of his campsite. No sense risking a forest fire. Once he sprouted fur he wouldn't need the extra warmth.

His groan turned into a growl as the pull of the moon took over. And the person who was Jason gave way to the wolf within.

* * * * *

The first thing Jason noticed when he woke the next morning was the temperature. It was considerably colder than before he'd shifted. The second thing was the snowstorm. It swirled around him, stinging his skin and catching in his eyelashes as he blinked toward the risen sun. He trembled, naked, in a wolf-sized dent of packed snow.

Fuck! The chains were gone and so was his campsite. He stood and turned in a circle but could barely see through the wild white blizzard around him. What he could make out, as he hugged his naked chest, was that he'd awakened on the side of a mountain, and several miles above him was the mouth of a cave.

He cursed again as he realized all of his gear, the silver cylinder Ryker had lent him, his phone, his clothes, everything he'd brought with him was back at the campsite, wherever that was. It seemed his wolf had escaped the chains and found the portal without him. Or else had been freed intentionally. He was betting the second. Nickelova wanted him weak. It was possible she wanted him dead.

Shivering, Jason began the painful climb toward the cave, teeth chattering in the storm. If he was lucky enough to make it there before freezing to death, he prayed the goddess would send him some ideas, because he had nothing to fight Nickelova with, aside from a lovesick heart and his two bare hands.

Reaching for a stone, he pulled himself up the ever-steepening side of the rock. His fingers and toes were bright red and hurt like a bitch. The pain in his extremities told him he was in trouble. Frostbite, for sure.

A quarter mile from his destination, bad turned to worse. He lost all feeling in his hands and feet, the tips of his fingers blackening. Not only could he no longer grip the side of the mountain, severe fatigue had set in, tempting him to curl up and fall asleep, a choice that would surely mean his death. But it was hopeless. His body could go no further. As the cold and the wind coaxed him toward unconsciousness, he closed his eyes and tried to meditate as Selene had taught him, to escape the pain by retreating to a place within his own head.

And then she was there, the bright blue light of Selene's soul on that plane of consciousness where they'd met before. "It's a trap," she said. "Nickelova is coming for you."

Was it real? Or a figment of his desperate imagination. Darkness closed in on him. He stopped fighting.

"I love you," he murmured. "And I'm sorry."

* * * * *

"Wake up, sleepyhead," Nickelova said. "You're no good to me dead."

Jason's body slapped the floor in front of a raging fire. He might have screamed if he had any control over his body at all. Unfortunately, that was not the case. He was conscious and in pain but physically immobile.

"Your wolf surprised me. After I freed him, he made it all the way to the vertical drop outside my cave before giving up. Much farther than I expected. Still, you are exactly in the state I hoped you'd be in when you arrived."

Slowly, painfully, Jason blinked his eyes, his warming limbs throbbing with pain.

Nickelova held a small vial over his lips. "A drop of fire lily juice can heal you, but before I give it to you, I need you to see who I have here with me." She yanked his chin to the side so he was facing a large pile of bones near the back of the cave.

Standing naked, her dirt-marred flesh shivering, Selene pressed her hands against an invisible barrier between them. Her butchered hair curled around her ears, rough-cut and matted. Jason tried to speak, tried to move to her, but he couldn't. His words were useless grunts.

"There, there, loverboy. We can talk about what happens to her next when you're better. It's all up to you. You decide her fate. But mark my words, if you betray my trust, it won't be you freezing to death outside my cave. It will be her."

With that, Nickelova tilted Jason's head back and administered a drop of healing elixir.

Warmth radiated from his stomach out to his extremities, thawing his frozen fingers and toes, and returning the blackening flesh to a ruddy hue. The process was painful, like burning from the inside out, but Jason welcomed the pain. He channeled every ounce of suffering into the dark place in his soul, the place he planned to draw on when he had the opportunity to rip Nickelova's heart out.

As the pain reached a crescendo, Jason's muscles spasmed. He curled on his side, his eyes catching on a glowing column of liquid entrenched in the stone wall on the far side of the cave. *What the hell?* Alex! He was naked, suspended inside like some sort of science experiment gone wrong. Eyes open, unblinking, he stared at Jason. Was he dead? Preserved? His body appeared to be healed. Why was Nickelova keeping him in that state?

Jason grunted and lifted a knuckle in Alex's direction.

"Oh, you found Alex. He's almost ready to return to us. Your sister's attack left him very near death, but I suspended him there, lung torn, liver split. He would have died without my intervention. That's a fire lily balm he's encased in. It's healed him from the inside out. I could revive him now, but I wanted to leave him where he is until you and I had a chance to… reconnect. Alex can be difficult. Jealous."

Stretching and contracting his hands, Jason tested his major muscle groups, rolling his neck as his body finished healing. He swallowed. Cleared his throat.

"I'm here now." Jason locked eyes with the beast in the red dress. "Let the girl go."

Nickelova gave a breathy chuckle, the edges of her pale hair catching in her sticky red lipstick as she leaned over him. "I can't let that happen. I need your loyalty and fidelity, Jason, and she's my leverage to make sure I get it."

Although everything inside him wanted to turn toward Selene, to swear his love and loyalty to her, he knew doing so would seal her fate. Her survival and his mission's success depended on convincing Nickelova to underestimate his feelings for Selene and to lower her guard. To trust him.

He was naked, weaponless, in the heart of the dragon's lair. But Selene had taught him that his soul was composed of great darkness as well as extraordinary light. He'd worked hard to get back to the light, to be good enough for Selene. But just now? This was a job for the darkness. He reached deep, calling up memories of Professor Matthews, of the dark days that once ruled his soul. Internally, he whistled for his wolf, loosed the vice he'd worked so hard the last month to suppress. Then he shielded his heart and did what he knew he had to do.

Composing himself, Jason rose to his feet, turning away from Alex to face Nickelova. Thank the goddess his back was to Selene. He wasn't sure he could do this if he could see her. He allowed his gaze to rake down Nickelova's face, linger on her breasts, her waist, and come to rest at the apex of her thighs. With some effort, he lifted one corner of his mouth, flashing the roguish smile he'd perfected over the years. He lowered his chin and looked at her through thick lashes.

"Why do you feel like you need her?" Jason said. "Haven't I always been a good doggie and come when you called?"

"Don't play me for the fool. I know what you feel for this girl. I felt it through our connection. Magic doesn't lie," Nickelova said through her teeth.

Jason approached her as he ran his gaze over her again. Closer, until his lips hovered next to hers and the back of his knuckles skimmed the front of her dress. "If your curse is so good at reading my feelings, tell me Nickelova, what am I feeling now?"

He almost cheered when he saw her lips part on an inhale and her thighs press together against the ache he presumed he'd started there. Before Jason had known what she was, he'd been a thorough and careful lover to Nickelova. He'd made her beg and scream. He prayed to the goddess that the catnip he'd planted was enough to lure her back.

"Hmmm." She looked down between them at Jason's naked body. "Is that for me?"

"Why don't you get a better look and find out?" he whispered. "And once you get a good look, you better taste it to see if it's your flavor."

She narrowed her eyes on him.

"I've missed you, Nickie." Jason pressed his lips to hers, the sticky feel of her lipstick smearing across his mouth. He forced himself to ignore the repulsion growing within him. He'd faked this before and he'd do it again if it meant Selene's life. He kissed Nickelova as if Selene's life depended on it, grabbed her hips, and ground himself into her belly.

Breaking the kiss, she panted, breathless, between them. "I knew you couldn't deny what we had together forever. You are more than simply a werewolf prince, Jason. You deserve to be alpha." She trailed her fingers under one of his nipples and down the hills and valleys of his abdomen. "When Alex wakes, you'll defeat him, force him to bow to you, then the three of us will take your pack and your society. And you will be alpha."

"You think *I* should call the shots instead of Alex?" This genuinely surprised him, until he thought about Alex's body in the jar. Alive or not, healed or not, he was obviously not the man he used to be. His body was likely weak after months of lack of movement, and who knew what kind of damage being jarred like a preserved frog might have done to his brain? He finally understood why Nickelova had wanted him here so badly. She needed him. There was no telling how much Alex there was left.

"Oh, I think you can rise to the occasion, and with my help, you'll have more power than you ever dreamed." She licked her lips.

"First things first," Jason said. "Where can we be alone? I want to show you how I reconnect."

"Right here isn't good enough for you?"

"There's no bed."

"You've never needed a bed before."

He sighed. "I don't like the audience."

"Afraid to upset the girl?" Nickelova asked with venom in her voice.

Jason forced himself not to look in Selene's direction and instead turned his gaze on Alex. "Actually, I was referring to your boyfriend. The way his eyes are open like he's watching us… it's creepy."

Nickelova frowned. "Hmm. He'll have to get used to the idea. No time like the present."

Jason cringed. "Are you telling me he's conscious in there? He can see us?"

"And hear us. He's in an altered state of consciousness but his senses still work. Everything is simply slowed down."

With a shake of his head, Jason tried to maintain his composure. He called on the wolf again, who growled and eyed his prey. "Privacy, Nickelova. Now!"

He was taking a risk speaking to her like that. He was defenseless and she could shred him with one pulse of her amulet. But he'd had enough experience with her to know she liked a man to take control. Nickelova was a dragon, but she was also all female. And Jason wasn't above using sex as a weapon. He stared her down.

"Come, my darling." She threaded her fingers into his and led him past Selene's cell. Jason glanced at her, just long enough to notice Selene's tear-stained face. He prayed to a goddess he didn't believe in that she'd catch on to what he was doing. *Trust me*, he thought. But there was no way to tell her. Nickelova turned a corner and they descended deeper into the mountain.

TWENTY-THREE

Selene wiped under her eyes. Had Jason just tried to send her a message? *Trust me.* The phrase had popped into her head. More likely it was a fabrication by her subconscious to try to convince her there was a reason for this nightmare.

When Jason had ignored her and approached Nickelova, she'd been devastated. Watching him kiss her had almost ripped her heart out. She didn't want to believe that Jason would turn on her so quickly, but she'd seen the darkness in him, knew what he was capable of. Jason and Nickelova had a history, a history that may be repeating itself.

The way Jason had looked at Nickelova was the same haunting way he'd looked at her that first day in his apartment and the time he'd almost lost control and she'd had to use her power against him. It was his wolf, his vice, back again from the graveyard of his past. Her first instinct was to believe he'd lost control.

But the more she thought about it, the more she wondered if Jason had more power over his wolf than she was giving him credit for. He'd arrived naked and alone. All he had at his disposal was his cunning, and his most practiced weapon within that arsenal was his ability to seduce. Was he truly attracted to Nickelova, or was he drawing her in, trying to earn her trust?

Her breathing slowed. Her tears dried. He'd found a way to lure Nickelova from the room, which meant she was alone. Alone for the first time since she'd been imprisoned here. Whirling, she scanned the pile of bones, looking for the sharpest one she could find. As she lifted it from the pile, she made a choice. She wouldn't think about or analyze what was going on wherever Nickelova had taken Jason. Instead, she'd devote all of her mental power to finding a way out. Today, she would not play the victim. Selene was a survivor.

Dragging the bone along the wall, she tested the confines of the space she was in. Three stone walls capped by a magical force that seemed impenetrable. But as Selene inspected the place where the magic met the stone, she found an irregularity in the surface. Digging her finger into the small opening, she was able to extend past the magical barrier. She picked up the bone and wedged the point into the hole, dislodging a chunk of rock the size of a fist.

As she brushed the rubble away and repositioned her tool, her gaze landed on Alex in his glowing amber tomb. His eyes were staring directly at her. Were they like that before? She'd recalled his eyes being closed. How much could he see from there? How aware was he?

Selene decided it didn't matter. For now, he wasn't a threat, and she had her work cut out for her.

TWENTY-FOUR

As inconspicuously as possible, Jason swept his gaze around the room where Nickelova led him, looking for anything sharp he could use to pry her heart out of her chest. There was a large bed dressed in oxblood linens and lacquered black furniture: including a dresser and nightstand, as well as a dressing screen decorated in a gold crane print.

"You must love red and black," he said.

"It's more than a preference. Red and black are the colors of my bloodline. They may not mean anything to you, but to me and my six siblings, they are the colors of home."

"Six?"

"Brothers. Dragons always lay seven eggs. Seven young. Females are rare. It's why there are so few of us."

"What do your brothers think of your plan to shack up with a werewolf and rule the world?"

She scoffed. "They don't understand. So few are evolved enough to look beyond their lineage." She rolled her shoulders back. "I don't want to talk about my family."

She scanned his naked body. He was still smudged with dirt and blood from his failed attempt to climb the mountain. "You need a bath," she said. With a pulse of her amulet, a tub of hot water appeared behind him.

Water. Ryker had said it weakened dragon fae magic. Jason hoped he was right. He stepped into the tub and lowered himself under the surface, mind racing. He needed a plan. *Think.*

She sat down on the upholstered bench at the end of the bed and crossed her legs, her spiky heel bobbing. "Now, tell me, Jason, why didn't you come to me sooner?" Her voice was loaded with cynicism.

Jason grabbed the soap and started scrubbing his chest, his arms, in an effort to buy time. A lie. He needed a lie, and it better be a good one. "Silas's friend is a witch. She detected your curse and broke it. After that, Silas locked me up. I've been on house arrest until now."

"Lies. You came for the girl. I know you did," Nickelova said.

"I was using the girl. I came for you."

"Liar."

Flashing a practiced smile, he looked directly at her and moved his hands to scrub his lower body. "You don't think I'm here for you?" One thing about Nickelova, her personality was predictably narcissistic. She would prefer to believe he was there for her, undoubtedly hold herself above a woman like Selene, and he planned to use that to his advantage.

She tipped her head back slightly, her lips parting, her nipples pearling behind the red material of her dress. Her eyes focused on the place where he touched himself beneath the water.

"We had some good times, didn't we Nickie? Those nights at Hunt Club?"

She uncrossed and re-crossed her legs, her cheeks coloring.

"You could join me," he drawled. "I could use some help in here."

She rose from her seat. Her arms slipped around his neck from behind. "You'd better not be toying with me, Jason Flynn. I won't be as forgiving next time."

"Next time. So you forgive me?"

She laid a violent kiss on his mouth in response. Suppressing the disgust that raged through his body, he nipped her bottom lip hard enough to draw blood. Under the guise of reaching for the zipper of her dress, he lifted his hands to her neck.

"Mmm," she moaned into his mouth.

He rose and forced her chest against his. The movement wasn't delicate. So close to the full moon, it would have injured a human woman. But just like old times, she went limp in his arms.

"Do you want this body?" she asked, bending backward, her lips grazing his.

"Not just your body, Nickie. I want your heart." He yanked the amulet over her head in one lithe move, tearing out a clump of her hair in his haste. She screamed. But by the time she could react, he was across the room and backing toward the door, the amulet dangling from his grip. He looped it around his own neck.

"You bastard," she shrieked, coming at him. "Don't you know that the amulet is useless unless I give you the power and the knowledge to use it?"

"I figured as much, but I'm more interested in keeping it from you than using it myself." He lowered his body, hands raised between them, ready to fight her if he had to. "If you're going to take me down, you're going to have to do it without magic."

Nickelova broke out in peals of laughter. "You fucking idiot. Do you know where the power of the amulet comes from? Dragon scale. And while I need it in my human form, scales are something I have all on my own."

As if she'd been hit by an ax, her skin split and her blood sprayed toward him only to be sucked back toward her shifting body. Gruesome round segments transformed into scales. She grew and changed in the most violent and grotesque transition he'd ever seen in a shifter. But as terrifying as the transition was, the end result almost knocked him on his ass.

A full-sized adult dragon hissed at him as he stumbled backward out the door, terror gripping his chest like a vice. She was bigger, deadlier in this form than he'd ever imagined. Her razor-sharp teeth gnashed in his direction. No wonder her family colors were red and black. Her scales glinted like bloodstained obsidian.

Scrambling out the door, he tore through the winding tunnel that led to the main chamber, thankful for his superhuman werewolf speed. The only advantage he had was the natural design of the passageway, which was narrow enough to slow the dragon down. It also served to partially conceal him from her slashing teeth.

A whoosh like a fireplace bellow came from behind him. *Oh shit!* He sprinted faster. Fire, hot and blazing, sprayed against the wall behind him, singeing his back. When he emerged into the main chamber, he dodged behind a large stalactite and desperately searched for something to use as a weapon.

"Jason!" Selene called.

He searched behind the invisible force field that capped her cell, finally finding her tucked into the far corner of the alcove. She'd chiseled a hole the size of her head in the section of stone at the far edge. "I'm sorry," he yelled. "I love you, Selene. It was the only thing I could think of." He pointed to the amulet hanging uselessly around his neck.

Nickelova cleared the stairwell, her claws clicking on the stone, sounding eerily similar to the click-clack of her high heels.

"Crap, she's big," Selene muttered, eyes wide.

"And breathes fire," Jason whispered back. "Got any ideas?"

The tapping claws stopped and the rushing of air started again. Jason pulled his shoulders in, trying to make himself as small as possible behind the stone formation.

Selene's gaze darted to the dragon and back to Jason. "Catch." She tossed a long, sharp bone through the hole. It skidded to a stop near his feet. He bent over to pick it up only to abandon that idea when fire blasted between them.

Head tucked under his arms, Jason avoided the worst of the flames, but still the smell of burning hair had him slapping out a spark near his temple.

"She stops moving when she blows," Selene said. "She's like a statue."

So that's what had given him the head start earlier. His werewolf speed was only part of his advantage. When she'd tried to fry him in the corridor, she'd had to stop to do so.

The flames abated and the clicking talons resumed. Selene jumped out from behind the stone and clapped her hands. "Hey you, hot mess! Yeah you, bitch. Over here!" She waved her hands. The dragon roared, advancing on Selene.

Jason rushed from his hiding place, sweeping the bone into his hand and skidding across the floor under the dragon. The dirt and grit bloodied his hip.

He looked up from his place between her legs, the dragon huffing in air again, her chest glowing crimson as she readied another blast of flames. With all his strength, he thrust the bone between the scales along her breast.

And failed at breaking her skin. A single scale popped off her torso and clattered beside him. The dragon, otherwise impervious to the sharp length of bone, bellowed a Jurassic Park worthy roar that reverberated through the cavern. He stabbed twice in the exposed spot, horrified when the point bounced off the leathery skin. The dragon turned a tight circle, trying to reposition its slashing jaws to reach him.

"Hey!" Selene yelled, tossing another bone through the hole she'd made in her cell. It was enough to distract the dragon for a split second, long enough for Jason to race from between its legs and around the room. There was no good place to hide but he flattened himself against the wall beside Alex's glass coffin.

Selene held up a meaty, rotting bone. "Come on. You want a snack? Come and get me!"

Nickelova struck at Selene, her snout bouncing off her own magical barrier. Jason's eyebrows shot up. Nickelova's dragon was not unlike his wolf. She was in there, for sure, but she didn't have the same human consciousness.

Selene waved the bone while the dragon scratched against her own magic, then sniffed the edges of Selene's cell, finding the hole she'd chiseled. *Uh oh.* The dragon dug its talons in, scratching and scraping at the opening until its snout could almost fit through the damn thing. If Jason didn't do something, Selene's might be the next set of bones on the pile.

Jason looked at the amulet around his neck, trying to will it to work. Nothing. He was on his own. "Hey, bitch! Anyone tell you that red makes you look bloated?" He waved his bone at the dragon. It worked. She turned from her Selene-under-glass dinner and stalked toward him, her wings flattening against her back.

Nickelova's reptile eyes locked on Jason and she froze. He watched her neck undulate with rapid swallows, the space around her heart reddening with heat.

"Fuck me!" Jason ducked and ran just as the fire rained against the wall he'd been pressed against. Red heat swallowed Alex's suspended body. A sharp crack marked a break in the barrier containing him, and Alex poured from the capsule onto the cave floor, slapping the rock like a dead fish. He did not move.

"Jason! This way. Climb through the hole," Selene yelled, pointing at the opening to her cell. He ran for it, just as the fire stopped and the dragon's wings pumped in an effort to pursue him. Nickelova's dragon stepped over Alex's body as if she didn't even see him.

Jason dug his fingers into a crag above the hole and thrust his legs through, but his shoulders caught on the uneven surface. "Fuck, what a time to regret gaining the weight back!" He reached his arms out, trying his best to collapse his shoulders.

Selene yanked on his hips and jabbed at the stone around his shoulders. The dragon eyed him, jaws open. If Jason didn't move, he'd have an upside-down, bent-backward view of his own death. He pushed against the stone, returning the way he'd come, and whirled to face the dragon's teeth.

"Stop, Nickelova," a low voice rasped from the center of the cave. The dragon's head whipped around.

Alex glistened in the firelight, his long, dirty-blond curls wet and clinging to his shoulders. "Yeah, it's me."

The dragon roared. Nickelova seemed confused about the reunion. She scratched at the floor and sniffed the air around Alex. He held up his hands toward her.

"Throw me the amulet, Jason," Alex said. "I'll free you. Nickelova's confused because I'm covered in her magic. She can't smell what I am. But as soon as I'm dry, I'm dragon fodder and so are you."

"Don't trust him," Selene said.

"Be reasonable, Jason. If she kills both of us, she'll simply find another wolf to do her bidding. She's always called the shots. She doesn't need me to bring her plan to fruition and she doesn't need you. I know how to use the amulet. I can save us both."

"Bullshit. You've never cared for anyone but yourself," Jason snapped.

Alex's eyes drifted to him. "What about you? Do you care about that girl behind you? You may not trust me, but I promise you, the amulet is our only hope of survival, and I'm the only one of the three of us who knows how to use it."

"And you promise to help us?" Jason said, eyeing the dragon.

The dragon snorted, a low growl rumbling behind the red and black glint of her scales.

"I promise. For the love of the goddess, our blood is my priority. We are both werewolves. We can work out our differences. Give me a chance to prove to you I've changed."

Alex couldn't be trusted. He was in league with the dragon, likely planning to give her the amulet in exchange for his own life. But as Selene crawled out of her prison behind him, Jason knew he couldn't save her on his own.

And then the dragon stilled, its throat swallowing and its chest glowing red with burgeoning flames. "Jason! I've been locked in a jar for months. I'll never outrun her. If you want to make it out of here alive, you'd best throw me that damned amulet!"

On impulse, Jason removed the amulet from his neck and tossed it to Alex.

"No!" Selene yelled from behind him. "What are you doing?"

TWENTY-FIVE

Flashing a wicked grin, Alex snatched the amulet from the air and looped it around his neck. The dragon's mouth opened and fire raged toward him. *Pulse.* The flames flowed around Alex as if he were safely locked inside an asbestos bubble.

When the dragon ran out of juice, Alex was left standing among whiffs of steam that curled from the floor. A deep, psychotic laugh echoed through the chamber. "Oh, my dear Nickelova, you have always been full of hot air."

The amulet pulsed again and Jason stared in disgust as the dragon was skinned alive. In a wave of angry screams, blood and gore and the break of bones, the reptile was transformed back into a woman. Nickelova lay helpless and naked at his feet, weeping in pain.

"You thought you could replace me." Alex spat in her face. "You fucking bitch." His foot connected with her ribs.

"You were weak. I thought you might die. I needed help to continue our plan," she whimpered.

He snorted. "Our. Plan. Key words, Nickelova. Do you know I could see and hear everything in that pickle jar you locked me inside? Don't lie to me. You wanted Jason from the start. Enjoyed his company a little too much when you were doing my dirty work at Hunt Club." He gripped a fistful of her hair and pulled her head off the ground only to slam it back into the floor.

"Hey!" Jason yelled. "If you're going to kill her, do it." He couldn't stand to watch him beat her, no matter what she'd done.

Nickelova's lips parted. "See? He's more of a man than you'll ever be."

Alex shook his head. "Ever since we were kids, all the ladies loved Jason. And who are you, sweetheart?" he said to Selene. "Flavor of the month?"

"Don't talk to her." Jason glared at him. "Don't even look at her."

"I'm a fair man," Alex said, his steely eyes flashing in the firelight like a madman's. "A man of my word. I told you I'd help you slay the dragon in exchange for the amulet, and here I am making good. Just one more thing to do." The amulet pulsed and Alex plunged his hand straight into Nickelova's chest.

For the rest of his life, Jason would remember the scream. Nickelova's mouth opened and a high-pitched shriek erupted from her lips, with an edge that seemed to slice right through him.

"By the goddess," Selene murmured. Out of the corner of his eye, he saw her turn away, unable to watch the horror happening before them.

Alex squeezed and pulled, the tear of flesh and crack of bone making Jason feel almost as ill as the painful gurgle that came from Nickelova's parted lips. The svelte blonde turned her face toward Jason and held out one hand in a plea for help.

"Please," she begged. But there was nothing Jason could do, even if he'd wanted to help the woman who'd threatened his pack, his love, and his life.

Alex tore Nickelova's heart from her chest, sending her toppling to the floor, writhing in pain. As he raised the heart above his head, blood ran in rivulets down his arm. The heart was not the soft, beating organ of a human, but a sparkling jewel, a gigantic red ruby that glinted between Alex's fingers in the firelight. A bright pulse at the center beat with a steady rhythm.

The wound in Nickelova's chest would have been fatal in any other creature, but not in a dragon fae.

"Look," Selene said, grabbing his hand.

The hole in Nickelova's chest filled, flesh knitting together magically. The bleeding stopped. The wound transformed from bright red to pale pink. Whimpering, she crawled away from Alex, curling into a ball against the far wall.

Alex's eyes fell on Jason and Selene. "I could kill you. With the smallest effort, I could shatter you like glass. But I'm a man of my word." He pointed at Nickelova. "She's mortal now. Kill her or leave her to die, I don't care. I don't need her anymore. But this makes us even. And next time I see you, Jason, all bets are off."

Alex headed for the mouth of the cave. Jason followed at a distance until both of them were staring out through the blowing snow. "It's almost nightfall," Alex said into the wind, not bothering to turn and look at Jason. "I wouldn't dally if I were you. If your wolf runs straight down the mountain, he might make the portal before it closes. Her mountain is in Siberia. The only reason you're here is because her magic transported you here. And I'm about to leave with her magic."

"You need to give us time to get out," Jason said. "I don't know the way. I'm not sure my wolf will know how to reach the portal."

Alex flashed a patronizing smile over his shoulder. "Sounds like you have a problem." The amulet pulsed, and he was gone.

Jason ran back into the main chamber and took Selene's hand. "We've got to go. The portal is closing."

"You'll never make it," Nickelova rasped, laughing in a way that seemed painful. "If you leave now you'll freeze to death before you reach the portal, and if you wait until you shift, you'll never make it before it closes."

Jason and Selene glanced toward each other and then at the slight, curled form leaning against the wall. Jason strode to her side and held out his hand. "Help us get out of here and I'll see you come to no harm."

Nickelova smiled sadly. "You are such a fucking hero, you know that?" She said the word hero like it was a curse. "I am not leaving this cave. And neither are you."

He grabbed her throat.

"Go ahead. Squeeze. What's one more death on your already tarnished soul?" She chuckled.

Selene's hand landed on his arm. "She's not worth it. She'll never make it out alive."

His grip tightened. He needed to kill her; it was too dangerous to leave her alive. But he couldn't do it in front of Selene, not with her looking at him like that. He released her neck and thought fast. Taking Selene's hand, he ran toward the passageway and descended to the bedroom where Nickelova had taken him before. "There must be a closet. She must have had gear for Alex, even if she had none for herself."

"Here!" Selene rummaged behind the folding screen. There was an entire set of brand new men's gear. Jason started dressing. Selene dug out yoga pants and a sweater that bagged on her less curvy figure, then donned a pair of snow pants. Jason handed her a puffy white parka.

"The zipper's broken," Selene said.

"I don't imagine she had cause to use it often."

"It's good enough." She shrugged into it. "There's nothing else." Hat, gloves, and boots later, they made their way toward the cave exit.

"You're not going to like this, but I need to kill her," Jason said. "Alex can control her now that he has her heart. It's not safe leaving her alive."

Selene raised her eyebrows. "What? Do you know this for sure?"

"Yes—what the fuck?" Jason balked as they turned the corner into the main chamber. A body-shaped cocoon had appeared where they'd left Nickelova.

"Dear goddess"—Selene's eyes went wide—"she's mummifying herself."

Through a silvery membrane, Jason could see Nickelova clinging to the dragon scale he'd plucked from her chest with his bone weapon. The same material the amulet was made of. Nickelova's eyes were closed and silver plates were shingling themselves over her from the feet up. Why hadn't he killed her when he had the chance?

Selene removed her glove and knocked her knuckles against the shell forming around the woman. The resulting ring of hollow metal filled the chamber. She glanced toward Jason. "What do we do?"

"We try to make it to the portal. Come on. We don't have much time."

* * * * *

As the sun sank in the arctic-blue sky, Selene followed Jason out of the mouth of the cave and into the burgeoning storm. They worked their way down the first drop, Jason helping her when her smaller body couldn't reach between handholds and footholds. The climb was nearly vertical, and she struggled to find her grip on the mountain in her boots and gloves. Struggled, until after thirty minutes of grueling effort, her grip failed. At the same time as she heard Jason call out, she dropped, skimming the icy stone and bumping down the side of the mountain.

"Ow! Ahhh!" Her insulated pants ripped and her shoulder smacked against a sharp crag. Sticky, warm blood oozed from the wound, but the ride didn't stop. Not until she slapped the side of the mountain where the slope leveled off with a back-cracking thump.

"Selene. Selene, are you all right?"

She could hardly hear Jason through the blowing wind. It was a painfully long time before he reached her and in those minutes, she concentrated on her breathing. In and out. The pain eventually numbed with the cold.

Finally, he was at her side. The snow stung her cheeks but it was her shoulder that worried her. It throbbed. She couldn't move her arm.

"You're bleeding," Jason said.

"I hit my shoulder." She tried to sit up, and a wave of pain and nausea forced her back down. "There's something wrong. I can't move it."

He took a closer look. When he rotated her wrist and tested her range of movement, she cried out. His face paled, and she knew it wasn't because of the dropping temperature. "I'm not a doctor but it looks dislocated to me."

"Or broken." She frowned toward the setting sun. "No time. Leave me. Find the portal."

"No," he said firmly.

"It's sundown. You can come back for me tomorrow."

"You'll be frozen to death by tomorrow."

"The shift will protect me. My wolf will be fine in this weather."

"And possibly lead you somewhere it's unsafe to shift back. If she can walk at all."

"Come on, Jason," she yelled, tears streaming now. "Don't fight me on this! We'll never make it out together. For once, just do the smart thing and go! I'm giving you permission to take the easy road."

He laughed and shook his head. "You spoiled me for that, Selene. I never want to do what's easy again. Only what's right. Only what you would do."

She leaned her head back against the rock, cursing.

"I think your shoulder is dislocated. I'm going to try to force it back into the socket."

"Do you know how to do that?"

"No. But how hard could it be?"

She looked at him worriedly. "Maybe you don't have to. Maybe it will correct itself when I shift."

"Maybe." Jason frowned. "But if it doesn't, I won't be able to correct it in wolf form."

"And if I can't move as a wolf, I'm dead."

"We're dead."

"Your wolf won't necessarily stay. It'll survive, any way it can."

Selene glanced at the mercilessly setting sun.

"It's going to work," Jason said resolutely. Gently, he worked her coat off her injured arm. She was still bleeding due to a nasty gash on the back of her shoulder. Hopefully that would heal when she shifted. And if Jason could knock the joint back into place, there was a shred of hope they'd make it out of here alive. He felt down her arm to the joint. Selene tried not to scream but the pain was nauseating.

"Just do it, Jason!" She could already feel the shift starting, a bubbling grind under her skin."

"I'm sorry about this." He positioned her arm again and gave a fast, hard thrust. This time Selene screamed, a scream that turned into a howl. The shift was coming. Her shoulder felt oddly warm, although her arm still wasn't working properly.

"Is it any better?" Jason pitched forward, the shift turning his green eyes to amber. He unzipped his jacket in the throes of transformation.

She used her good hand to strip out of the winter clothes, following his lead. "I still can't move it, but it doesn't hurt as much." She pitched forward, her jaw elongating as the snow stung her naked flesh.

"I love you, Selene," Jason said suddenly, claws sprouting from his knuckles. His distorted hands landed on the stones near his feet.

"I didn't believe you before," she said, the need to confess gripping her heart. "I thought I was just another passing fancy, temporary entertainment for your vice."

"That's not true."

"When you left with Nickelova tonight, I thought you were joining up with her. I thought you couldn't resist her."

He shook his head. "I had to—" He groaned as tawny fur broke out across his inner arms.

"I said yes before on Rivergate grounds because I wanted you so badly I was willing to lose everything, even if I might have you for only a short time," she rambled. She had to tell him, had to get it out. "I never thought I could want someone again. I thought I was ruined for love after what happened to me… the things I did. But I believe you now. I love you too, Jason, in a forever way." White fur climbed her arms, over her shoulders, between her breasts.

If Jason said anything else, she didn't hear it. Her last thoughts were that she wasn't cold anymore. And then the wolf took over and she wasn't Selene anymore.

TWENTY-SIX

The white wolf's consciousness was one-part instinct, one-part chemistry, and one-part body language. With a soul of total freedom, she sped down the mountain, ignoring the slight ache in her shoulder that gave her a pronounced limp. The dark wolf, her pack, was by her side, smelling of thick fur and hunger. Yes, hunger. It was time to hunt.

She whimpered and the dark wolf with the tawny belly licked her face before scanning the mountain for movement; a rabbit or bird would be a fine meal. Her leathery nose opened and sniffed the air. There was something on the wind. Exotic. Close. The dark wolf must have smelled it too because his head snapped around.

The source of the smell came from a bird, a huge bird that flapped its gigantic black wings in the blowing snow. The wolves stalked forward, hunting the black thing that folded and snapped in the wind. All at once the black wings expanded, then settled like a heavy fog around the form of a woman. The white wolf stopped. This was not food. This was danger and power. With jet-black hair and a dress that seemed to hold itself up by magic alone, the woman pinned the wolves with her icy blue stare.

"My good and faithful daughter," she said, approaching. "Do not be afraid." The white wolf bowed to the woman, a deep instinct driving her to revere what she didn't fully understand. The woman's hand came to rest on the wolf's head. "You must follow me now. This place is no longer safe for you."

The dark-haired woman turned and strode down the mountain, the wolves heeling at her side. Miles passed. The white wolf's stomach growled, but she did not stray from the one who led her away. The darker wolf whimpered. He was her alpha and the whine made her nervous, but the pull the mysterious woman had over both of them trumped pack hierarchy. They followed with an instinctual trust.

And then a ripple cut through the night, constricting quickly as if the darkness was a closing mouth.

"Come, daughter. Bring your love. I will hold it open for you." The woman pulled back the corner of the night sky and motioned for the wolves to pass through. The dark wolf leapt through first, disappearing somewhere into the beyond. The white wolf stepped forward and licked the woman's hand.

"You are welcome, dear one. Now, you must go. You've done me a service. Go reap your reward."

The wolf raised her paws to jump through but paused when a man appeared across from the woman, a man with thick twisting horns that grew from the sides of his head.

"Meddling again in the fate of this world, Hecate? I might think you weren't taking our agreement seriously," the horned man said. He was hulking and horrifying. His mere presence made the white wolf shiver.

The woman's gaze shifted to the white wolf. "Go. Now!"

The wolf leapt through the portal, feet leaving snow but landing on bright green grass. When she turned around, the woman's fingers retracted from the tear in the darkness. The white wolf stared at the place she'd just entered through. There was something she should remember, something important. But a moment later, the portal was gone.

A moment after that, the memory of the portal grew distant and faded entirely. All there was in the world was the dark wolf, who jogged to her side with a bloody rabbit between his teeth.

* * * * *

Bright, warm light pierced Jason's closed eyelids, but he fought the urge to wake up. He was happy. Worn out, muscles sore, he relished the after-shift euphoria, his body flooded with endorphins counteracting the last shift of the month. He stretched hard and lean in the soft grass, rolling onto his side.

And then, with a start, he remembered. The mountain, the storm, Selene. He opened his eyes and frantically searched for her. But he needn't look far. She was right beside him, curled into his side as if she still had a tail. He stroked the short strands of her hair back from her face and ran his hands down her naked body, searching for injuries. The gash on the back of her shoulder was already a pink scar. Everything else looked okay.

"I like this way of saying good morning," she whispered, rolling into his embrace.

"We made it. Oh thank the goddess, we made it." Jason exhaled. "How's your shoulder?"

"It's fine. You fixed me. And I think the goddess is exactly who we have to thank."

"Hmm?" Jason was distracted by the way her body shifted under his as if it was something she'd done every day of her waking life. She rolled him on top of her and wrapped her legs around his hips. He balanced on his elbows so that he wouldn't crush her.

"I have a memory, a wolf memory. It's a slippery thing, like a forgotten dream, but I seem to remember the goddess, Hecate, showing us the way out. Do you remember that?"

Jason shook his head. "No. I think I remember catching a rabbit."

She laughed beneath him and the jiggle of her body did all sorts of things to his libido. His erection kicked against her lower belly. "Selene… I love you."

"I love you too." She looked into his eyes. They were nose to nose and chest to chest, but it was the connection between them that made it the most intimate position he'd ever been in with a woman.

"You once told me that the only way to conquer a vice is to discover the need it's trying to fill and fill it with something else."

She nodded. "An anchor, a feeling or experience that fills you with light and keeps you from the darkness. We found yours. The memory of your family when you were all together."

"The thing is…" He stroked her hair back, taking his time to choose his words carefully. "I don't think that memory is strong enough to anchor me anymore."

"No?"

"No. That memory is marred with darkness, with loss, with regret," he said. "But I have one that is strong enough. A new memory."

He met her gaze, that violet blue as intense as he'd ever seen it. "When I was in that room with Nickelova, there was a moment when I felt my vice fighting for control. I needed an anchor, and when I closed my eyes, all I saw was you. You are a light to my soul. Our love is bright enough to stave off the darkness, pure enough to be the only anchor I'll ever need."

"It's okay if you hold the memory of your parents above me. It's not a competition. They loved you first," she said seriously.

"Yes. Yes. I'll never forget them or that perfect day you reminded me of. But an anchor, an anchor should be powerful enough to root your soul. You are that thing for me now. I may be able to exist without you, Selene, but I can't live, not really."

"What are you saying?"

"I don't just want you to move out of Sanctuary, I want you to move in with me. I want to wine you and dine you and fly you around the world and dance with you in my kitchen every night. I want to give you all the experiences you never had growing up. And in time, when you are sick of dating me, I want to marry you."

Selene's mouth dropped open, a confused smile flashing briefly. "What?"

"Say yes, Selene. Say you'll be mine and only mine, for always."

Her mouth worked but no sound came out. Jason started to wonder if her answer was no. He pulled back slightly, unsure if he should remove his hand from where it rested on her ribs. But her expression didn't say no. It lifted and lighted from within.

"Yes. Yes, Jason." Her voice was thready. "I'll be your anchor. I'll be your anchor because you've become mine." She grabbed his face and pulled it to hers, her lips parting to let his kiss in.

Jason wanted their first time to be special. Dinner, flowers, candlelight, hours of worshiping every inch of her creamy flesh. Not in the forest after a near-death experience. But Selene had other plans. He thought she'd be hesitant, maybe scared, considering her history. He was wrong. She grabbed his hips and demanded his full and undivided attention.

"Are you… sure…?" he stuttered. "Oh. Game on."

He'd been with women before, hundreds of women actually, but as he connected with her, he realized he'd been deceived. All the sex he'd had in the past had been plastic imitations of the real thing. The intimate connection he held in his arms blew every other experience away.

Working his arm under the small of her back, he lifted her, supporting her beneath him as he worked a better angle. She hooked her ankles behind him and wrapped her arms around his neck, clinging to him. The scent of mango and vanilla wafted from her skin. He buried his face in what remained of her hair.

She thrust up against him. "Harder. I won't break."

He lifted her, guiding her until he was balanced on his knees with her straddling his hips. Deeper this way, he held nothing back, reveling in the tiny moans she produced with each targeted thrust. Selene's violet eyes sparked with passion as she came crashing down on him in a wave of flawless skin and delicate bones. He moved inside her, allowing her to wash over him, to draw him higher, to the peak, to the place he was tempted to tumble over.

"Oh no, not yet," she said, slowing her movements. "I want more."

He held himself back, circling his hips to keep from going over the edge. Cupping her under the thighs, he lifted, standing from the soft grass and supporting her against his chest. The trunk of the tree they'd woken under made a fine brace for one foot, his hand resting on the trunk. In this position, he was so deep inside her, he feared he'd hurt her. But she only gripped him tighter, scoring his back with her nails. He didn't hold back.

She moaned in his ear, pulling on his shoulders to ride the rhythm. He lost himself in her, in the connection that was everything he always wanted and never knew he was missing.

* * * * *

Selene met Jason thrust for thrust, her arms straining to draw him closer, her abs working to build the momentum, her mouth melding with his until she'd explored every inch of his mouth and neck. And still she wanted more.

For all the times she could remember having sex, it was never like this. Never filled her both emotionally and physically. Her body could not contain the love he poured into her. She was a bowl overflowing with light, a light that shone in all her dark corners, smoothed her jagged edges, and made her feel like all the pain of the past served a purpose—to bring her to this point of total ecstasy.

His body pounded into her, but it was the way he looked at her that sent her over the edge. There was nothing short of reverence in his eyes. She leaned her head back and came apart, shattering in his arms with his mouth to her neck and his hot skin against hers, his arms the only thing holding her up.

She felt his orgasm like a rush within her and the effect was intense. Her body clenched around him, spilling over with pleasure once more until she clung to him through the aftershocks. They came together in a way that made her lose where she ended and he began, and she clung to him as he stroked the sparks that flared within her.

After a long time, she slid off his body and onto her own feet. "By the goddess," she whispered.

Jason rested his forehead against hers. "By the goddess, indeed."

They were still recovering when a sound came on the wind.

"Jason!" A man's voice called from a distance. Selene looked around the tree in the direction of the noise. Silas, Laina, and Gerty were headed toward them.

"Hmm." He smiled down at her. "Looks like we've been rescued."

TWENTY-SEVEN

"He has her heart?" Laina cried.

Jason placed a finger over his lips when the patrons of the coffee shop where they'd chosen to meet turned to stare at their table. Dressed and rested, he and Selene had met with Silas and Laina to fill them in on what had happened.

"What were you thinking, Jason? How could you hand over the amulet like that?" Silas kept his voice low, but Jason had no trouble hearing the venom in it.

"He had no choice, Silas. Jason couldn't use the amulet. It takes some kind of… additional magic or experience," Selene said. "We were naked, trapped in a dragon's lair on the side of a mountain in Siberia. If Jason had let Nickelova fry Alex, we would have been next."

"And believe me," Jason said, "I thought about falling on my sword for the pack. But once Nickie killed us, she'd have the amulet back. It was only a matter of time before she'd find another werewolf to take Alex's place."

"But, she's dead, right?" Laina asked.

Jason ran a hand over his face. "No. Not exactly."

Selene wrapped her fingers around Jason's forearm and squeezed. "Nickelova didn't die when Alex removed her heart; she became mortal. We could have killed her… but we thought we needed her to get back through the portal. By the time we realized what she was doing, it was too late."

Silas rubbed his temples and sighed deeply. "What was she doing?"

"During the fight," Jason said, "I dislodged a scale from her dragon form. She used it to form some kind of cocoon around herself."

Silas growled. "So not only is Alex still at large, but Nickelova is a ticking time bomb in a mountain somewhere."

"How much do you want to bet that Alex returns her heart to her at some point and wakes her up? I imagine a girl will do a lot for a heart," Laina said.

"I'm sorry." Jason glanced at Selene.

She squeezed his hand in support, narrowing a hard stare on his brother and sister. The look she gave Silas alone could solder iron. "I don't have any family. But if I did, I think I'd be a lot happier to have them home safely." Selene shifted her gaze, pointing a finger at Laina's nose. "Your brother almost died last night."

Silas sighed. "We're happy to have you back. Both of you. But this changes everything. As alpha, I'm just a little nervous about what this means for the pack. We may need to go into hiding again."

"No," Laina said. "Not again." Tears pooled in her eyes. "Kyle and I have just started to make a life for ourselves. He finally has new clients for his treehouse business. I can't ask him to trash everything he's worked for and I certainly can't close Four Paws again."

"I'll talk to Grateful and see if there's anything we can do to strengthen the wards around Rivergate," Silas said. "I'm disappointed Nickelova could see and hear these two from beyond the boundary. We've got to protect ourselves."

"I'll talk to Gerty," Laina said. "If Nickelova leveraged the curse she had on Jason to find him, maybe she knows how to make sure Alex can't use that in the future now that he has her heart."

There was a long silence. Jason stared into his coffee, tapping out a song on the side of his cup. Part of him agreed with Silas that he'd put the pack in danger when he pursued Nickelova on his own. But as he glanced at Selene, the steam from her coffee curling along the fine bones of her jaw, all he could think was he'd do it again.

Silas cleared his throat and stared pointedly at Jason and Selene's coupled hands. "Not to be the chaperone at the dance who taste tests the punch, but it seems like there's another topic of conversation that needs to be broached. What's going on with you two?"

* * * * *

"I'll be forever grateful for what you did for me, Artemis," Selene said as she packed up her room into the same brown plaid bag she'd used since childhood. "I'm sorry if I was a disappointment."

"A disappointment? You?" Artemis raised her eyebrows. "Never. *I* could never be disappointed in you. But do you know who you have disappointed?"

"Who?"

"All the Fireborn families with girls Jason's age. They've had to say good-bye to the dream that their daughters might one day snare a spot as the next princess. He's taken. Permanently."

Selene sighed. "I didn't set out with a goal of loving Jason. It just happened. It crept up on me like some wonderful dream as if one moment I was drifting to sleep and the next I was in his arms."

"What causes people to fall in love? Is it chemistry? Opportunity? The hand of the goddess herself?" Artemis wrapped an arm around her shoulders and squeezed. "All we know for sure is that love is precious and should not be denied."

"It's frightening, though. I'm leaving the only life I've ever really known and loved behind, to go shack up with a guy who just recently recovered from a major addiction. It sounds crazy when I say it out loud."

The older woman smiled. "One must be brave to truly love. What you set out to do is not easy work. It's not magic. Loving someone is seeing them for who they truly are, the light and the dark, and inviting all of it, the whole person, into your life unconditionally. You can leave or protect yourself if things go wrong, Selene, but true love will stay with you. It will be a beacon that leads you back to him again and again. You'll always demand the best of him, always pick him up when he falls, always ask the goddess to protect him, and he'll do the same for you if he truly loves you."

Selene nodded, a memory blowing into her thoughts like a cool breeze. "Speaking of the goddess, I had a strange experience I need to ask you about."

Artemis folded into a chair at the small table in her dormitory. Selene sat across from her and rested her coupled hands on the table. "What is it?"

"When Jason and I were escaping from Nickelova's lair, I was in wolf form, but I swear I remember seeing the goddess lead us to safety."

"What did she look like?"

"Tall, curvy, with long waves of wild black hair and a dress that clung like a black fog around her, as if it was cut from the night itself. The wind had no effect on her—it didn't even rustle her hair. And although Jason and I had almost frozen to death before the shift, she didn't seem cold at all. She called me her dear one."

"That certainly sounds like the goddess."

"She led us to the portal, but before I could pass through, I noticed a man standing across from her."

Artemis stiffened. "What sort of man?"

"A man with large twisting horns growing from his head, like a ram but different, straighter, not as curly. He was naked from the waist up. Hairy. And his eyes were black and dull as coal. He told her she was interfering and that was against their agreement."

Artemis stood and paced the small room.

"I don't usually remember things from my wolf form. I'm wondering if my brain simply produced this to fill in the gaps of an emotionally trying night. It couldn't possibly have been real."

"Oh, I fear what you saw was quite real. In fact, I'm sure of it."

"How?"

Artemis frowned. "We don't teach of the horned god here. There's no way you could describe him as perfectly as you have without seeing him firsthand."

"The horned god?"

"He goes by many names but in our tradition, he is called Panaal." Artemis spread her hands. "All existence must maintain balance."

"Of course. The goddess demands balance in all things."

"Not just the goddess. Everything. From the largest beast to the tiniest cell, balance is the most fundamental of laws. Disrupt the balance and things start to evolve. Everything, all the interdependencies of life begin to change, to adapt until a new balance is found. Panaal is the balance to Hecate, the masculine to her feminine, the keeper of the underworld."

Selene's shoulders drooped. "I don't understand. I thought Hecate was her own balance. The maiden, the mother, and the crone. Protector of women. Goddess of the crossroads. Mother to all supernatural beings."

"If Hecate is all about balance and order, Panaal is all about the wild, about chaos, about man's primal needs. He is the source of the raw instincts that drive us all in the absence of intelligence and civilization. He is the hunter where our goddess is healer. He thrives on disorder. He desires turmoil. He loves war."

"Sounds like a real ball of fun," Selene said, swallowing. "What do you think it means that he was in my memory?"

"I'm not sure, but I don't think it's a coincidence that he arrived after Alex took Nickelova's heart. If Hecate is the mother of werewolves, Panaal is the father of dragons."

"So when Alex and Nickelova were working together there was balance?"

"But now a werewolf has a dragon heart, and the goddess has helped you escape almost certain death."

"Is it just me, or does this situation make your spine tingle?" Selene asked.

Artemis shivered. "I fear that heart has far greater value than the amulet Alex had before and far greater consequences for our pack."

TWENTY-EIGHT

Outside the monastery, Selene smiled when she saw Jason waiting for her, parked in the sleek sports car she thought looked like a drivable piece of art. He rolled down the passenger's side window as she approached and sneered at her brown plaid bag.

"Are you sure you want to bring that thing? I thought I'd take you shopping today to replace everything inside it."

"Everything?"

"Everything you'll let me… with the exception of that navy-blue number you wore when you made me cookies. We'll keep it for sentimental reasons."

"I think I'll keep all of it," she said through a smug smile. "For sentimental reasons."

He climbed out and lifted the bag from her hands, snorting when all her worldly possessions fit easily in the Bugatti's meager trunk space. He hurried to open the door for her, then climbed behind the wheel.

"I have one quick stop to see a client before lunch. Are you game for Valentine's restaurant?"

"I've never been," she said truthfully.

He straightened in the leather seat like the idea was sacrilege. "Oh, Selene, we must rectify this situation. Chef Logan Valentine makes a chocolate cake that will positively light your fire." His eyes raked down the torso of her plain gray dress.

With one raised eyebrow, she stroked down her leg and allowed her fingers to tug her hem up to midthigh. "Too late."

Jason's smile faded to a darker expression as his gaze caressed her thigh. But he didn't touch her. Instead, he started the engine and drove away from the monastery, merging onto the road that led into the city. Had he lost interest in her already? Her gaze drifted out the window as the car sped forward, embarrassment warming her cheeks. What was she thinking? This wasn't the time or the place.

But then his hand was on her inner thigh, his palm caressing north, pulling her dress even higher. "I didn't think Artemis would enjoy the show. She was watching you through the upstairs window."

"Oh," she said. The word turned into a moan as his fingers found her center, rubbing over her simple cotton underwear.

"You're wet already. I've barely gotten started."

She moved against his hand, grinding into his fingers until he repositioned to oblige her. What was it about the way he touched her that incinerated all former rationality? She'd gone years without sex and now could think of nothing but Jason and making up for lost time. Selene whimpered and ran a hand between her breasts.

A passing car honked and Jason overcorrected the wheel. "I better pull over before I kill someone. Has anyone ever told you, you're very distracting?"

"Never." She smiled at him and licked her lips. He overcorrected again.

Both hands firmly on the wheel, Jason took the next exit, but Selene wasn't in the mood for waiting. She'd waited long enough for her true love, for a relationship where she could safely express herself sexually. She didn't plan to wait another minute.

She reached over and unzipped his fly, freeing his erection and sliding her fingers along his shaft.

"Selene," he murmured.

She leaned over, ducking her head beneath his elbow and taking his cock into her mouth. She'd never done this before in a car. Never done anything like this before on purpose, driven by her own desires. She relished it, sucking and licking—the power she had over him—as he began to moan her name in earnest.

The car stopped, but Selene didn't. She hastened the rhythm, feeding off the rush of his breathing and the way he slapped the ceiling of the car. She watched him writhe out of the corner of her eye as she mercilessly drove his cock into the back of her throat.

And then he shattered. She swallowed what he gave her, savoring the command she had of his body. He was hers. Putty in her hands. Her lids sank as the tremors rippled through him and he looked at her like she made the world spin simply by breathing.

"By the goddess, Selene, you are full of surprises."

"Just making up for lost time." She grinned.

She slid back into her own seat. "Holy mother of pearl!" Selene almost hit the roof. A figure stood in front of their car in the alley where Jason had parked. The menacing form hovered in the shadow of the building, almost blending into the darkness.

"It's okay. It's Ryker."

"He wasn't watching, was he?"

Jason zipped his pants. "Well, he wasn't there when I parked the car."

Heat flooded Selene's cheeks.

"Believe me, there's nothing to be embarrassed about. This guy has seen worse. Way worse."

She straightened her dress and climbed out of the car. Ryker moved toward them, his forward momentum out of sync with his actual steps as if he were traveling a moving walkway.

"Jason… so glad to see you survived your encounter with your jaded dragon lover." Although Ryker spoke to Jason, his eyes never left Selene. He stared at her, entranced, licking his lips occasionally.

"Er, thanks," Jason said awkwardly.

"Nice to… see you again," Selene said, almost sputtering.

Ryker's dark eyes flashed red. "It is my sincere pleasure." The man brought his full lips to the back of her hand, her skin heating where the kiss connected. She rubbed the area, which itched like it had endured a minor burn. "And, may I say, the shorter style suits you." He gestured toward her hair.

Selene ran a hand through the sleek pixie cut she'd gotten to even out her butchered hair. She wasn't sure she'd keep it, but it was nice to know someone appreciated the look.

"Have you heard the news? Selene is no longer an acolyte; she's my fiancée." Jason drew her against his side and away from Ryker.

"Fiancée?" He licked his lips. "This *is* a happy turn of events. Come inside," he said. "I assume you've brought me something."

Jason patted the pocket of his suit jacket and nodded.

Ryker turned the corner and entered the shop Selene had visited before. Daylight had done nothing to reduce the creepiness of Lost Things. The antique sign squeaked on its hinges above her head, and she noticed what looked like a new, smaller human skull in the window display.

"What exactly do you sell here, Ryker?" she asked curiously. "I didn't ask you before."

"No. You were too busy threatening my life in exchange for finding your man."

Selene frowned.

"Ah, never mind. The excuse to set foot in Soleil's brothel was payment enough for my services." He lowered his voice. "She doesn't care for me."

"Personality conflict?" Selene asked.

"As an incubus, I feed off sexual energy. The clients might not notice, but it drains the girls." He smiled wickedly. "Thank you, by the way. For earlier." He gestured in the direction their car was parked. "And they say there's no such thing as a free lunch."

Selene felt her cheeks blaze with the hot sting of a blush.

He approached her, inhaling deeply. When he spoke again, his voice was flinty and his breath carried a hint of sulfur. "To answer your first question, I am a purveyor of antiquities: rare magical objects and forgotten and out-of-print texts on the supernatural. Feel free to examine the merchandise, but don't touch. Some of my inventory can be… temperamental."

She nodded slowly. "Wouldn't dream of it." She focused on a dehydrated monkey's paw.

"Now, Jason." Ryker held out one hand, displaying long tapered fingers with nails filed to a point.

Jason removed a silver cylinder from his pocket and placed it in Ryker's palm.

"What is this?"

"This is the weapon that you lent me. I was unable to use it."

"Our agreement, Jason, was that I would lend you this enchanted weapon in exchange for a dragon's heart. Are you telling me you did not uphold your end of the bargain?"

"I'm saying I wasn't able to use your weapon, and thus, I didn't get the heart. I'm returning the weapon."

"Where is the heart?"

Jason narrowed his eyes. "What makes you believe it's not still beating in Nickelova's chest?"

Selene wouldn't have thought it possible but Ryker's expression darkened even further. The incubus gave off an aura that was both the darkest red she'd ever encountered and cold as ice. Cold fire. That's how she'd describe him. A wild, icy absence of humanity.

"I can *feel* it." His voice was harsh. "You don't have it with you, but it's close. Very close. Did you hide it from me? Did you think I wouldn't know?"

Jason's eyes widened. "You feel it now? Here?"

"Since early this morning." Ryker rubbed a circle over the left side of his chest. "The air is thick with it, a heady perfume of power that makes my skin tingle."

"Alex Bloodright stole that heart," Jason said. "Do you think you can lead us to it? He'll be where the heart is."

Ryker examined Jason and then Selene. "You're telling the truth."

"Of course I'm telling the truth. I'd give you the heart if I had it, but Alex took it. If he's here, we need to stop him."

Ryker sniffed the air. He stepped out of the store, the door chiming above their heads, and turned slowly on the sidewalk. His tattoo glowed through the right sleeve of his shirt, the round curves and geometric shapes of an ancient symbol glowing through the posh fabric. "I thought you were hiding the heart from me for your own purposes."

"I never had the heart. Alex killed Nickelova and left us to die. We barely made it out alive."

Ryker assessed Jason, his upturned eyes blazing. "Very well. I'll lead you to the heart." Ryker extended his hand. "Alex is yours. But the heart is mine."

"And then we're square?"

Ryker nodded.

"Deal." Jason shook the demon's hand. Selene had a bad feeling about this. Was it a good idea to make a deal with a demon?

Ryker motioned for them to follow as he drifted down the street in that unusually fluid way he moved, turning left down the next alley.

"Was that a good idea?" Selene whispered to Jason. "He's a demon, like from the underworld. How do you know he's not manipulating you?"

"He's not from the underworld. He's from New Jersey," Jason whispered.

"Huh?"

"His mother was human." He glanced in her direction. "I gave him the loan to start Lost Things. We got to know each other."

"Can we trust him? He almost killed you with that snake ring."

Jason took a deep breath and let it out through his nose. "Ryker's help is often complicated. But he's an incredibly useful friend to have."

"By the goddess." Selene lowered her chin and squeezed Jason's hand harder.

"This is the vampire district. Why would Alex come here?" Jason mused.

"It's the middle of the day. Most of the local residents are sleeping," Selene said. "If he came earlier this morning, there's no place safer."

"Or a vampire is helping him," Jason said.

Ryker looked both ways before climbing three stairs to reach the entrance to an apartment complex. He sniffed, then tried the door—locked. Selene perused the intercom system, noting it was labeled with symbols instead of names.

"Don't bother," Ryker said to her. "Everyone who lives here is snug inside their coffin for the day, with the exception of the man you're looking for, and I'd rather not call his attention to our presence."

"So how do we get in?" Jason asked.

Ryker's brow puckered, that wicked grin turning his full lips. With a twist of his neck, his entire body transformed into a column of smoke that filtered under the door and reformed inside. He unlocked and opened the door for them.

"That must come in handy," Selene said.

The demon held a long tapered finger to his lips. "Shhh." They followed him up the stairs, Selene rolling her footsteps to keep them as quiet as possible. Jason did the same. Ryker's feet never seemed to fully make contact with the floor.

When they reached apartment 5A, Ryker stopped, inhaling deeply. He glanced at Jason and did the disappearing smoke act again. The lock clicked slowly and the door opened.

Jason motioned to Selene to wait where she was. She shook her head. Not a chance. They drifted into the apartment, but it was completely empty. Not so much as a chair in the main room.

Selene turned to Jason in confusion and caught a streak of blue move out from behind the door. "Look out!"

Alex's joined hands pounded the back of Jason's skull, sending him toppling forward. Instead of falling flat on his stomach, Jason tucked and rolled. Selene shuffled out of the way as Ryker blew through

Alex like a dark wind and disappeared. So much for a show of solidarity. While Alex shook off the sting of sulfur, Selene went for the amulet. She planted her bare foot on his stomach, snatched the dragon scale, and lifted. It slid over his head easily enough, but his hand shot out and caught the chain.

"Not yours, wolf bitch." Alex sneered at her before wrapping his hand in the chain and yanking, hard. Her slight weight tumbled into the wall.

Jason jumped onto Alex's back, his bigger size dwarfing the rogue wolf's sickly physique. One, two quick punches to the werewolf's temple and Jason had him by the throat. Alex spun away and stumbled backward toward the window, holding his neck with one hand and his side with the other.

"Still hurting, Alex?" Jason asked, approaching slowly. "Maybe you needed another month in Nickelova's pickle jar. I don't have one of those for you to heal in, but the pack has a nice strong prison cell."

Alex donned the amulet again. "I could kill you, blow you apart. But we worked together to fight Nickelova, Jason. We'd be stronger if we joined forces now. I don't want to hurt you."

Selene focused in on a bead of sweat at Alex's temple. It rolled down the side of his face, followed by another. His muscles twitched like he could barely hold himself up.

"You *can't* hurt us," Selene said. "Not without hurting yourself even more."

Alex took a step back.

"All magic comes with a price. Using that amulet costs you, and judging by your appearance, you've paid a high price the last couple of days. You're even more emaciated than you were only days ago. You might be able to use magic against us, but the process could kill you."

Jason took another step forward. "Where's the heart?"

Baring his teeth, Alex said, "Somewhere safe."

A black mist collected between them. Ryker. He held up the throbbing red jewel Selene knew was Nickelova's heart. "Mmm hmm. Yes. It was in a safe, hidden under the floorboards in the bedroom." The incubus grinned. "Finders keepers." He glanced between Alex and Jason, his barbed tail sweeping the air behind him.

"No!" Alex cried and dove for the heart. Ryker gave him a patronizing wave before dissolving from within his arms, heart and all.

Jason used the distraction to his advantage. He plowed his shoulder into Alex with a righteous howl. They scuffled toward the window where Alex gripped Jason by the shoulders and yanked.

"Watch out!" Selene screamed, but it was too late. Glass shattered. The two wolves tumbled through the fifth story window.

Selene ran to the edge, searching the sidewalk below. Alex was gone, and Jason lay facedown on the concrete. "Oh no, Jason!"

TWENTY-NINE

Selene thundered down the steps loud enough to wake the dead. Luckily, if any of the undead in the apartments did wake, they didn't bother emerging from their afternoon's rest. She raced to Jason's side, just as he was pushing himself up off the concrete.

"Are you hurt? Maybe you shouldn't move." Glancing up at the hole that was the fifth-floor window, she examined his body, searching for signs of injury.

"I'm okay." Jason rolled over, pushing himself up on one elbow. "Alex used the amulet to break his fall before he blinked out of here. I only fell a couple of feet. It didn't feel good but I'm not damaged."

"Thank the goddess." Selene pressed a hand to her chest.

"Silas isn't going to be happy to learn Alex got away again." Jason ran a hand through his hair in frustration.

"Silas needs to count his blessings. By the look of Alex's aura, he's going to be underground for a while. The man was sick. Very, very sick."

"Yeah?"

"His entire being was surrounded by a dirty gray halo. He wasn't completely healed. My guess is that he'll be searching for a healer to finish what Nickelova started. He's not strong enough to go far. Silas will find him. Plus, thanks to you, Alex no longer has Nickelova's heart."

Jason's face fell. "Speaking of the heart…" He rose from the concrete and took her hand, pulling her in the direction of Lost Things. He called Ryker's name as soon as he walked through the door.

"Back so soon?" The demon appeared between two piles of antique crap, looking quite pleased with himself.

"No thanks to you."

"What part of our agreement led you to believe I'd help you kill Alex?"

Jason shook his head. "The heart…"

"Is mine. That was our agreement."

"What do you plan to do with it?"

Ryker gave a knowing smile. "Save it for a rainy day. A treasure like that could be dangerous in the wrong hands. I intend to keep it in the right ones. Mine." He flourished his fingers in the air.

Jason nodded. "I trust you'll let me know if anything changes in that department. No matter what Alex or anyone else offers you, give me a chance to top it before you let it go."

Ryker looked confused for a moment, then answered in a slow and steady tone. "The heart is not for sale, Mr. Flynn. I plan to keep it for my own purposes. But I want you to know, I cherish our relationship and won't let it fall into the wrong hands. You can count on me to keep it safe. Now, can I interest you in a gift for your lovely new mate? Perhaps a candle that tells your future in its smoke?" He lifted a black wax taper from a pile beside him.

"No," Selene said firmly, pulling Jason toward the door. "Thank you, Ryker, but we have to go."

"Very well. A pleasure to see you again, Selene. Good luck with your new… situation."

The door chimed as it closed behind them and they headed, hand in hand, back to the car.

* * * * *

"One more bite?" Jason held a forkful of Valentine's chocolate cake in front of Selene's lips, his hand cupped beneath her mouth to keep any crumbs from falling onto the sheets. After an afternoon of shopping, they'd stopped at their now-favorite restaurant, Valentine's, for dinner to go.

"Ugh, it's delicious, but I couldn't eat another bite," Selene said.

It had been two days since he'd tackled Alex through the window—two days since they'd moved in together—and Jason couldn't remember ever being happier.

"I love to watch you eat."

"Really?" She laughed.

"Really. The thought of providing for you is oddly satisfying." He leaned over her, stroking the delicate space between her eye and her cheekbone with the back of his fingers. "I want to give you the best of everything until the shine coming off of you tells everyone you're mine."

Selene glanced around the room at the dozens of packages lined up against the wall of their bedroom. "The things you buy me won't say I'm yours." She laughed when his face fell in horror. "But I will. I'll tell everyone."

He kissed her softly. "I like that. I plan to do the same. Speaking of telling people, I was thinking we could get married next summer, in Italy. We can go there first. Soon. Find the perfect place."

"Italy? But… I need to find a job. I'm not an acolyte anymore. I thought you could help me choose a new career."

He lifted his eyebrows. "You don't have to work if you don't want to."

"I want to! I have to have something to do while you're doing what you do."

His face turned serious and he gave her a long hard look. "What is it that you're passionate about?" In all his years as an investor, he'd learned the most successful careers and companies were based on passion. He wouldn't let her settle for anything less.

She stared at the ceiling for a moment. "Other than studying the goddess, I'd have to say baking. I love to bake."

Jason gave her an ear-to-ear grin. "Perfect. My company will fund your bakery start-up. Step one: research other bakeries. I recommend we start in Italy, perhaps with a side trip to a culinary school in France."

She giggled. "Italy. What a coincidence." She shrugged. "Fine. I guess I have to start somewhere."

"Me too." He kissed her neck in earnest.

"Haven't you had enough?" Selene joked as his lips worked their way down her body once more.

He stopped and locked eyes with her, allowing all levity to bleed from his expression. For days he'd analyzed his wolf, waiting for his vice to return with a vengeance. Waiting to want another woman so badly that he'd have to lock himself in his bedroom again to stop from hurting Selene. But that day hadn't come. All he wanted, all his wolf wanted, was her.

"Yes and no," he said. She quirked an eyebrow. "Yes, *you* are enough for me. Just you. Forever."

She smiled sheepishly. "And no?"

"No, I have not had enough… of you."

She squealed with joy as he pulled her beneath him once more, her body quickly melding with his. Threading his fingers into hers above her head he dedicated himself to making her believe she was the only woman in his universe.

EPILOGUE

Silas sat at the bar in Valentine's restaurant, sipping his vodka and tonic and trying hard to forget that Alex was back in Carlton City. With the dragon fae amulet in his possession again, no one was safe. Sometimes being a detective and the alpha responsible for Fireborn pack was like bailing a boat with a large hole in the bottom. As soon as he thought he'd done what was necessary to keep his wolves safe, something would happen and they'd be at risk again. And nothing he could do as their leader or as a member of the Carlton City PD could help.

He didn't blame Jason for what happened. If he'd had to choose between Nickelova or Alex, he'd have chosen Alex too. What was that old saying? Out of the frying pan, into the fire? As a werewolf, Alex was the less threatening option, with or without the amulet. Not to mention, according to Jason, he was still recovering from his injuries. With the right help, Silas knew he could track Alex down and end this war for good.

"The answers you're looking for aren't at the bottom of that glass," Soleil purred into his ear.

When had she arrived? Standing behind him, her presence put off a sunny glow in the dim light, her radiant heat warming his back. "I came as soon as I heard."

She slid onto the leather seat of the stool next to him with the grace of a dancer. Everything about her was long and polished, down to the golden blond chignon that crowned her head. His stomach twisted from holding back his desire for her. For a moment, he flashed back to the last time he'd had her in his bed, the alcohol fueling a vivid recall of the warmth of her skin and the soft feel of her body. He squirmed on his stool and focused on his glass.

"Have you heard anything? Any sign of Alex?" he asked her.

"No. I've spoken with all the girls. He hasn't come into the bordello. With dragon fae magic, he might be able to conceal his appearance, but as you know, what makes Maison des Étoilles extraordinary is my girls can read our patrons' thoughts, their deepest and truest desires."

"I remember," he said. His eyes betrayed him and he looked at her again, his gaze tracing the deep vee of her royal blue wrap dress. It tied at her waist with a bow that Silas desperately wanted to pull. He forced his attention back to his drink and cleared the thickness from his throat. "He's weak. Not visibly injured, but emaciated. In need of care. Jason doesn't think he could have gone far."

"I see. Probably in no need of sex then." She narrowed her blue eyes. "He'll go underground. You said he was last seen in the vampire district?"

"Yes. Just north of Lost Things."

"Interesting. I haven't heard a thing, which means…"

"Someone must be helping him."

"A vampire?"

"Seems likely. Most vampires have no moral qualms about hosting a murderer, especially in trade for daylight services. A werewolf watchdog while you're in the coffin would be more than fair payment for hiding, feeding, and healing."

"Vampires aren't traditionally healers," Soleil said.

"Not per se, but vampire blood has healing properties for various supernaturals."

"It also has side effects."

Silas nodded, taking a swig of his drink. "Use too much blood and he'll bind himself to the vampire. Alex will become the bloodsucker's pet if he's not careful."

"It's more likely he'll try to find a witch or dark fae to do the healing, even under a vampire's protection." Soleil frowned. "I'll do some research and bring you a list of underground healers."

"Thanks, Sol."

She turned her attention fully on him. "How are you handling all this?" When she crossed her legs and leaned toward him on the bar stool, the slit of her dress fell to either side of her knee and gave him an eyeful. *Repeat the alphabet. Think of teddy bears.* He rolled his eyes toward the ceiling.

"The empty glass isn't enough of a clue?"

"You're welcome in my room anytime, you know, if you need to work off some of that stress. I've missed you."

And now his erection was straining against his fly with a vengeance. "There are nights I dream of taking you up on that offer," he said, trying not to look at her. "But I meant what I said."

"You want exclusivity."

"I'm a man and I'm an alpha. I don't like to share."

"And I'm a madam of a bordello. Sharing is my business."

"You run the place, Soleil. It's not as if you're the one for hire."

"I've seen many males, human and supernatural, cross through my doors. Trust me when I tell you, monogamy is a disease. I love you too much to curse you with it."

"And I love you too much to give you anything less." With that he did allow his gaze to meet hers, her dark blue eyes reflecting the light from the bottles behind the bar. Her irises reminded him of the star-filled night sky.

"I didn't come here to fight," she said. "I came to try to help. A dragon's heart is a powerful weapon in the wrong hands."

Silas sighed. "Well, that is one problem solved. Ryker *found* Nickelova's heart while my brother Jason was pounding Alex's face. Alex got away with the dragon scale amulet, but the heart is safe with Ryker."

She lifted an eyebrow. "If you consider that yard sale of a shop Ryker runs safe. Although a demon would never give up a prize like that, not for all the money in the world."

"No?"

Soleil looked at him incredulously. "Unlike us, demons and dragon fae are made of the same stuff. They originated with the horned god, Panaal. It is said that a demon with a dragon's heart is impervious to the usual things that can kill a demon: a seraph blade, holy water, and burning the bones of the human body he was birthed from."

Silas swirled the ice in his glass. "I guess I don't know much about demons."

"Take my word for it, Ryker will wear that thing around his neck if he can find a locket it will fit in. And he'll never let it out of his possession."

"As long as it's out of Alex's hands, I'm going to count that as a win."

She reached out to run her nails through the back of his hair. The feeling sent goose bumps dancing across his skin and a zing of electricity through his body. He closed his eyes. "You're the smartest man I've ever known. You'll figure this out. I know you will."

Her fingers trailed from his neck and her lips landed on his cheek, her fresh-as-sunrise scent filling his lungs. He opened his eyes in time to see her crossing to the door.

"I'll bring you a list of healers as soon as I can get it," she said.

"Thank you." His voice was all gravel.

With a small wave goodbye, she allowed the door to close behind her.

She was right. Silas would catch up to Alex. He had to. After what Alex had done to his parents, his siblings, and his pack, Silas owed him vengeance. He wouldn't be able to sleep until Alex was a pile of bones. He was a talented detective. It was only a matter of time.

Why then, as a detective, an alpha, and the smartest man she had ever known, could he not solve the mystery of Soleil's heart? He motioned to the bartender to refill his vodka and tonic. There may not be any answers at the bottom of the glass, but tonight he was going to keep drinking.

At least until he ran out of questions.

For now, that was all he had.

ABOUT THE AUTHOR

Genevieve Jack is a registered nurse turned author of weird, witty, and wicked-hot paranormal romance. Coffee and wine are her biofuel, the love lives of vampires, shifters, and witches her favorite topic of conversation. She harbors a passion for old cemeteries and ghost tours, thanks to her years at a high school rumored to be haunted. Although she calls the Midwest home, her heart belongs to the beaches of the Southeast, where she spends her days with her laptop and one lazy dog.

Do you know Jack? Join my reader list for exclusive content, sneak peeks, and giveaways available nowhere else. http://smarturl.it/KnowJackNews

79459980R00180

Made in the USA
San Bernardino, CA
15 June 2018